Part One

Canvas of Unity

Echoes of Tomorrow

Michael A. Garcia

Published by Nexa Novels, 2023.

ECHOES OF TOMORROW

First edition. September 15, 2023.

ISBN: 979-8223118435

Written by Michael A. Garcia.

Table of Contents

Dedication

"To Mom and Dad,

This novel is a labor of love, a tapestry woven from the threads of your wisdom, your guidance, and your boundless love. From the stories you shared by the fireplace to the life lessons etched in the lines of your smiles, you have been my greatest inspiration.

Mom, your unwavering belief in the power of dreams, your resilience in the face of adversity, and your nurturing spirit have shaped the characters in these pages. Your warmth and love are reflected in every embrace, every kind word, and every act of compassion within these chapters.

Dad, your strength, your unwavering principles, and your boundless curiosity have given life to the heroes and heroines of this story. Your wisdom and the lessons you've imparted through the years are the guiding stars that light their paths.

In every page, in every word, and in every sentence, your love and influence are woven into the very fabric of this tale. This novel is a tribute to the extraordinary parents who taught me that the greatest stories are those written with love, courage, and the belief that anything is possible.

With all my heart,

Your Son Michael.

CHAPTER ONE

Lost in Tomorrow

The cityscape of NeoVille was a symphony of lights, sounds, and motion. Hovering vehicles zipped through air-lanes, colossal digital billboards beamed advertisements and news, and drones flitted about like mechanical fireflies. In the midst of this, Central Park stood as a serene oasis—a blend of nature and tech, with trees whose leaves shimmered with bioluminescent glow and holographic birds that sang in perfect harmony.

Liam sat on a park bench, his eyes scanning an augmented reality (AR) sketchpad, a faint outline of NeoVille's skyline emerging from it. But today, his usual enthusiasm for painting was replaced by a sense of disconnection. Memories of past mistakes, of a graffiti incident that went too far, weighed heavily on him. NeoVille was home, but he felt adrift, lost in its expansive tomorrow.

A soft chime alerted him to a message. Aria, his best friend, was inviting him to a tech exhibition. He hesitated, then decided to go. If anyone could pull him out of his funk, it was Aria.

At the exhibition, innovations from across the globe were on display. There were virtual reality ecosystems, smart textiles that changed patterns with moods, and AI-guided art tools. Yet, amidst the marvels, Aria led him to a simple, unassuming booth.

"This," she said, pointing to a blank digital canvas, "is your way back."

Liam was puzzled. "It's... empty."

Aria's eyes sparkled with mischief. "Exactly! It's a collaborative canvas. People from all over can add to it, creating a mosaic of stories. What if you took this concept and made it bigger? A mural for NeoVille, a canvas that tells our collective story."

Liam's heart raced. The idea was audacious, yet it resonated with something deep within. A way to redeem himself, to reconnect with NeoVille, and to be part of its vibrant tapestry.

Liam and Aria, side by side, staring at the blank canvas. It wasn't just an empty screen; it was an invitation to dream, to create, and to find one's place in the sprawling narrative of NeoVille.

CHAPTER TWO

Dive into VirtuReal

The whirlwind of colors around Liam slowed to a tranquil mix of pastel hues, and he found himself standing in a vast, open field. Giant blossoms floated overhead, and the grass below rippled like the waves of a gentle sea.

"This...this is incredible, Ari," Liam breathed, his fingers itching to capture the beauty he was witnessing.

"That's the magic of VirtuReal," Aria said with a smirk. "Your mind merges with the digital realm. These colors, the scenery—it's a reflection of your inner emotions and thoughts."

Liam took a hesitant step forward, the grass lighting up with each footfall. "So, this is all... me?"

"In a way, yes," Aria replied. "It reacts to you. Think of something, anything, and watch."

Closing his eyes, Liam thought of a bird, remembering the sketches he'd made as a child. Suddenly, a flurry of luminescent birds emerged, their wings shimmering and tails trailing sparks of light. They circled around him, their harmonious chirps creating a melody.

A laugh escaped Liam's lips, a genuine, heartfelt sound that he hadn't heard from himself in ages. "It's magnificent."

Aria watched him with a satisfied expression. "But remember, VirtuReal is a tool. It won't give you inspiration, but it can help you find it."

Liam looked at her, realization dawning. "It's not just about painting what I see. It's about understanding what I feel."

"Exactly!" Aria beamed, grabbing his hand. "Now, come on. There's much more to explore."

The pair ventured deeper, encountering a labyrinth made of crystalline walls reflecting memories from Liam's past—some joyous, some painful. As they navigated through, Liam started to understand; his blockage wasn't due to a lack of creativity, but rather a reservoir of unprocessed feelings.

At the heart of the labyrinth was a serene pond. Liam's reflection, younger and full of zeal, stared back at him. It was a reminder of simpler times when the world's complexities hadn't muddled his passions.

"You see," Aria whispered, leaning on his shoulder, "sometimes, to move forward, we need to look back, accept who we were, and embrace who we're becoming."

As they exited VirtuReal, Liam felt a weight lifted. NeoVille might be changing, but so was he. And with Aria by his side, he felt ready to blend his essence with the evolving world.

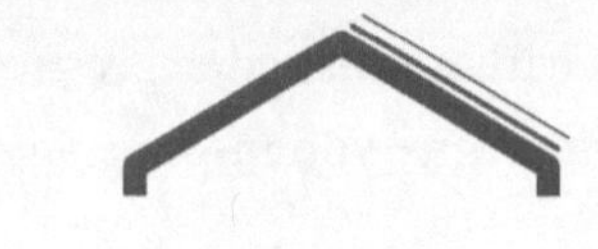

CHAPTER THREE

Echoes of Yesterday

Back in the tangible world of NeoVille, the sun was setting, casting a warm, orange hue over the towering skyscrapers. Liam and Aria sat on his apartment's balcony, cups of herbal tea warming their hands.

"It's overwhelming," Liam admitted, taking a sip. "The weight of emotions I've been carrying, the memories I'd buried. VirtuReal made me face them."

Aria nudged him gently, "But you weren't alone."

He smiled, looking at her. "Never am, am I?"

She shrugged, "That's what best friends are for. Though, I didn't expect VirtuReal to take you down such a deep memory lane."

Liam chuckled, "Me neither. But it wasn't just the past. I saw potential futures, ideas, dreams I'd forgotten about."

Aria raised an eyebrow, intrigued. "Like what?"

"Like the mural I'd always dreamt of painting on the side of this building," Liam gestured to the stark gray exterior of his apartment complex. "A fusion of the old world and the new. A depiction of NeoVille's heart and soul."

Aria's eyes sparkled with excitement. "Why not do it?"

He hesitated, "It's a massive project. Plus, the city council..."

She waved him off, "Leave that to me. I've got a few connections. We can get the permits."

Liam looked at her, a mix of gratitude and surprise. "You're serious?"

"As a system crash," she quipped, a cheeky reference to an old tech joke.

The two of them spent the evening planning, sketching, and discussing the mural. It was ambitious, but for the first time in years, Liam felt his passion reignited.

The mural would be more than just paint on a wall. It would be a declaration—a statement that even amidst the relentless march of technology, the human spirit, with its memories, dreams, and emotions, remained unyielding.

The night grew darker, and NeoVille's lights began to shine brighter, reflecting off the intricate web of overhead transport lanes and digital billboards. But on that balcony, two young souls were shining even brighter, dreaming of a project that could change their lives and the city they called home.

CHAPTER FOUR

Brushstrokes and Bytes

Over the next few days, Liam's apartment transformed into a bustling studio. Sketches and digital blueprints adorned the walls, while drones, programmed by Aria, hovered around, capturing 3D models of the building's exterior.

Liam often found himself working late into the night, fingers stained with digital ink and charcoal. For the mural's design, he envisioned the harmony of nature and tech—tree roots morphing into circuitry, birds with wings of shimmering holograms, and humans with hearts glowing like LEDs.

Aria, meanwhile, was busy liaising with the city council. With her relentless spirit and a knack for persuasion, she managed to secure a meeting with NeoVille's Art and Culture Commissioner.

On the day of the presentation, they entered the NeoVille Municipal Hall, a massive structure with walls that seemed to breathe, adapting colors based on the moods of the room. They were directed to a conference room where a holographic table awaited them.

"Liam, Aria," greeted Commissioner Rhea Nash, a stern-looking woman with silver streaks in her hair. "I've heard a lot about your proposal. Show me what you've got."

Aria gave Liam an encouraging nod. With a deep breath, he activated his AR wristband, projecting the mural design onto the table. It sprang to life, a moving tapestry of colors and stories.

"As NeoVille progresses," Liam began, "it's easy to lose ourselves in the binary of the past and future. This mural is a bridge. A celebration of where we've been and where we're going."

Rhea studied the design intently, her face giving away no emotion. After what felt like an eternity, she finally spoke, "It's audacious. It's bold. And it's exactly what this city needs. You have my approval."

Aria and Liam exchanged elated glances, barely able to contain their excitement.

"But," Rhea added, causing their hearts to momentarily drop, "ensure that the community is involved. Let them add their brushstrokes. Make it a collective masterpiece."

Liam nodded in agreement, "Absolutely, Commissioner. We want this to be a mural by NeoVille, for NeoVille."

As they left the Municipal Hall, they were met with a crowd of reporters, their drones hovering and flashing, capturing their reactions. Word had spread quickly.

"This is just the beginning, isn't it?" Aria whispered to Liam as they were swarmed by the media.

He grinned, "Indeed. Let's paint our future."

CHAPTER FIVE

Canvases of the Community

Word of the mural project spread like wildfire through NeoVille, invigorating both the digital forums and the physical streets. Everywhere Liam went, he was met with curious eyes and eager hands, each wishing to be a part of this groundbreaking endeavor.

Aria, ever the tech whiz, set up a digital platform called "NeoMural" where residents could contribute ideas, sketches, and stories they wanted the mural to represent. The response was overwhelming. Thousands uploaded their visions, memories of ancestors, hopes for the future, and moments that defined NeoVille for them.

One afternoon, as Liam scrolled through the entries, he came across a sketch by a 10-year-old girl named Mia. It depicted a young child holding hands with a robot, their fingers intertwining in a dance of flesh and metal. The caption read, "My best friend isn't human, but he has the biggest heart." It was a simple, yet powerful testament to the harmony between technology and humanity in NeoVille.

Another moving contribution was from an elderly man, showcasing the city's evolution. His drawing displayed NeoVille as a tiny settlement, transitioning through the ages to its current grandeur. His note read, "I've seen this city grow. Brick by brick, byte by byte."

Inspired, Liam decided to host a series of community workshops. Open-air tents were erected in NeoVille's Central Park. Easels, digital drawing tablets, brushes, and paint cans were lined up, beckoning all to share their stories. People of all ages poured in, their excitement palpable.

Aria oversaw the tech side, helping people digitize their drawings or using AR to project their ideas on virtual walls. Liam, on the other hand, provided guidance, often getting lost in deep conversations about art, history, and the soul of NeoVille.

As days turned into evenings, the park became a luminous spectacle. Drones hovered, capturing moments, while the soft glow from holographic projections painted the night. Music played, food stalls offered futuristic delicacies, and laughter echoed—Central Park was alive in celebration.

On the last day of the workshops, as the sun cast its golden hue over the city, Liam stood atop a small platform, addressing the crowd.

"NeoVille," he began, his voice choked with emotion, "I started this project thinking it was my story I was painting. But this... this is *our* story. This mural will be a testament to our collective spirit."

Aria joined him, her hand on his shoulder. "Together," she added, "we'll make NeoVille not just a city of the future, but a city of its people."

The crowd erupted in applause, their faces glowing with pride and anticipation. The canvas was set, and the masterpiece awaited.

CHAPTER SIX

Digital Dilemmas

The heart of NeoVille was abuzz with excitement, but with the rise of any great endeavor, challenges are inevitable. Aria had been spending hours in her makeshift tech hub in Liam's apartment, sifting through the flood of contributions on NeoMural. However, not all uploads were in the spirit of collaboration.

One morning, as the first rays of the sun streamed through the windows, Aria discovered that NeoMural had been hacked. Numerous spams and derogatory messages had flooded the platform, and some genuine contributions had been maliciously altered.

Liam found Aria hunched over her workstation, frustration evident on her face. "What happened?" he asked, taking in the chaotic screen displays.

"Somebody doesn't want our project to succeed," she muttered, her fingers flying over the keyboard, trying to trace the source of the breach.

Liam felt a pang of anxiety. "Can we recover the original uploads?"

Aria sighed, "I've backed up most of them, but some recent ones might be lost. The bigger issue is the negative PR. People might lose trust in the project."

Just then, a notification popped up on Liam's AR glasses. It was from NeoNews, NeoVille's top news aggregator. The headline read: "NeoMural Hacked: A Stain on NeoVille's Unity Project?"

Liam's heart sank. They had been making such positive progress, and this setback threatened to overshadow their hard work. "We need to address this publicly," he declared.

Aria nodded in agreement. "And we need to reinforce our digital defenses. This can't happen again."

The duo called an emergency town hall meeting at Central Park. A massive crowd gathered, their faces reflecting a mix of concern, curiosity, and determination. The giant digital screen showcased the corrupted and genuine versions of various artworks.

Liam stepped up, taking a deep breath. "NeoVille, our unity has been challenged. But we won't be deterred. Our mural, our story, is bigger than any digital disruption."

Aria projected a visualization tracing the hack's origins. "The breach has been contained. We're strengthening our defenses and setting up a community-driven moderation system."

A voice from the crowd called out, "What if they come back?"

Aria smiled confidently, "Then we'll be ready. NeoVille's tech community is unmatched. I invite coders, hackers, and cybersecurity experts to join us in fortifying NeoMural."

The response was immediate. Dozens stepped forward, ready to volunteer their skills. The incident, instead of becoming a breaking point, was turning into a rallying cry for the community.

As the evening wore on, NeoMural was not only restored but became more robust and secure than ever. It was a testament to

NeoVille's spirit – in the face of adversity, they chose unity and resilience.

CHAPTER SEVEN

Shaded Past, Colorful Future

While NeoMural's digital troubles were on the mend, a different storm was brewing for Liam. In the midst of the mural's growing popularity, a NeoVille journalist named Calla Mercer started digging into Liam's past, unearthing stories and memories Liam had long wished to keep buried.

One evening, as Liam was sketching out a portion of the mural, he received a message on his AR glasses: "Exclusive: The Troubled Past of NeoVille's Mural Maestro - by Calla Mercer."

Dread filled Liam as he scanned the article. It spoke of his tumultuous teenage years, a time filled with rebellion, misplaced anger, and art used as an escape. The report detailed a particular incident where a younger Liam had been involved in defacing a historical monument with graffiti.

Aria, upon seeing the article, rushed to Liam's side. "Liam, talk to me," she said, concern evident in her voice.

He took a deep breath, "I was young, angry, and lost. Art was my only solace, but I didn't always use it right."

Aria squeezed his hand. "Everyone has a past. But it's what you do now that defines you."

But the damage was done. The story became the talk of NeoVille. Some criticized, questioning the decision to let Liam lead such a monumental project. Others empathized, recalling their own youthful misjudgments.

Feeling the weight of the public's scrutiny, Liam decided to address the situation head-on. He called for a gathering at Central Park, the same place that had witnessed the birth of the mural idea and their collective unity against the digital hack.

With Aria by his side, Liam faced the crowd. His voice trembled, but his resolve was firm. "Yes, I made mistakes. I regret them deeply. But NeoVille gave me a chance to change, to grow. This mural isn't just about celebrating our city's spirit; it's also my way of giving back, of making amends."

A hushed silence enveloped the park. After what felt like an eternity, an elderly woman stepped forward. "I remember the monument," she said softly, "but I also remember seeing a young boy, days later, trying to clean the paint off it, tears in his eyes."

The crowd turned to her, listening intently.

"That boy was Liam," she continued. "We all deserve second chances. Let's not taint our future by denying our capacity for change."

The atmosphere shifted palpably. What started as a gathering filled with skepticism turned into one of understanding and support.

As the day faded, the large screen in Central Park lit up, showcasing designs for the mural - a testament to a city ready to paint over its prejudices and embrace a brighter, unified tomorrow.

CHAPTER EIGHT

The Artist's Awakening

In the following days, Liam's life became a juxtaposition of emotions. Support from the community came in waves, but so did whispers and sideways glances from skeptics. Though Aria and many others stood by him, the weight of his past lingered, adding a somber hue to his vibrant world.

One evening, as the sun set casting long shadows over NeoVille, Liam found himself wandering the city's old district, away from the augmented reality screens, the drone-filled skies, and the bustling tech hubs. Here, the remnants of the old world stood tall, a testament to a time when things were simpler.

He stumbled upon an old art gallery, 'Timeless Tales'. The rustic sign and faded paint seemed out of place in a city that prided itself on futuristic flair. Curiosity piqued, Liam entered.

The gallery was a haven of classical art. Paintings from the Renaissance, intricate sculptures, and avant-garde pieces from the 20th century filled the space. As he walked, each art piece seemed to whisper tales of artists long gone—tales of their triumphs, despairs, revolutions, and redemptions.

In a secluded corner, Liam found an easel with a half-finished painting. It depicted NeoVille—but a version untouched by time, where cobblestone streets met towering skyscrapers, and children with AR glasses played beside elders recounting tales of yore.

Beside the easel stood an elderly artist, her hands stained with paint, eyes reflecting wisdom. "Ah, you found my little project," she said with a smile.

Liam was captivated. "It's beautiful. It's like you've bridged centuries."

The artist chuckled. "Art has a way of doing that. I've lived long enough to see the world change, but through my art, I've always tried to remember our roots."

Liam hesitated before asking, "Have you ever doubted your art? Felt like it was all for nothing?"

The artist looked at him thoughtfully. "Many times. But art isn't just about the good days or the praises. It's also about the struggles, the critiques, the days when you feel lost. That's what gives it depth."

Liam looked down, taking a moment before admitting, "I'm the one behind the NeoMural project. And right now, I feel lost."

The artist moved closer, placing a reassuring hand on his shoulder. "Young man, art is transformative. Not just for those who view it but for those who create it. Your mural will be your redemption, your bridge between past mistakes and future promise."

As Liam left 'Timeless Tales' that evening, he felt a renewed sense of purpose. The weight of the past was still there, but now, there was also hope, inspiration, and a drive to create something timeless.

CHAPTER NINE

Collaborative Canvases

With renewed vigor and determination, Liam returned to the NeoMural project. But he realized that the mural wasn't just his redemption story; it was NeoVille's collective tapestry, interwoven with threads of individual experiences, dreams, and hopes.

He approached Aria with an idea: "What if we set up multiple collaborative zones across NeoVille? Spaces where people can come, share their stories, and directly contribute to the mural."

Aria's eyes lit up. "Physical and digital spaces combined! We could use AR to let people see their contributions in real-time."

And so, NeoMural Collaboration Zones were born. Spread across the city, these zones became melting pots of creativity. Residents, young and old, tech-savvy, and traditional, came together to paint, draw, code, and narrate.

A local school transformed its playground into a storytelling haven. Here, children narrated tales of their NeoVille, while artists translated them into sketches, and tech enthusiasts digitized them on the spot. An old cafe in the historic district hosted sessions where elders shared memories of NeoVille's past, infusing the mural with rich history.

The most touching moment came when the elderly artist from 'Timeless Tales', Ms. Eleanor, hosted a workshop. She spoke of NeoVille's evolution, drawing parallels with art movements over centuries. At the end of her session, she added her rendition of the cityscape to the mural, seamlessly blending the old with the new.

The Collaboration Zones broke down barriers. People who had previously been skeptical or distant from the project found themselves immersed. The mural became a living entity, growing and evolving with each passing day.

Amidst this collaborative spirit, Aria organized a surprise for Liam. One evening, she led him to a secluded zone, where a group of teenagers were working on a section of the mural. It depicted a young boy, paintbrush in hand, standing before a vast canvas, with shadows of his past behind him and a radiant city ahead.

Liam, recognizing the metaphor, was overwhelmed. Aria whispered, "This is your chapter in NeoVille's story. But remember, it's just one among many."

CHAPTER TEN

Dawn Before Daylight

As the days melted into nights and nights bloomed into days, NeoVille's skyline was slowly transforming. The NeoMural, no longer just a project but a living tapestry, was nearing completion. The anticipation in the air was palpable.

Liam and Aria stood atop a building overlooking the city, a holographic mini-version of the mural displayed before them. Sections of the city were pulsating with lights, indicating the active Collaboration Zones.

"It's beautiful, isn't it?" Aria mused, "Not just the mural, but the journey. From a single idea in Central Park to a city-wide movement."

Liam nodded, lost in thought. "It's more than I ever imagined. But it's also daunting. Once this is complete, it will be open for the world to see."

Aria looked at him, sensing the weight of responsibility he felt. "And they will see not just a mural, but the heart and soul of NeoVille. Our unity, our struggles, our dreams."

There was a gentle chime in Liam's AR glasses. It was a reminder for the grand meeting scheduled the next day, where representatives from every Collaboration Zone would gather. They would discuss the official unveiling, the global press invites, and the augmented reality tours planned for the mural's premiere.

But alongside the logistical details, there was an underlying current of excitement. Rumors were swirling about international artists and tech innovators wanting to join the unveiling, turning it into a global event. NeoVille was about to be thrust into the global spotlight.

Just as they were about to leave, a soft shimmer caught Liam's eye. Floating down from the sky was a tiny, illuminated drone. It landed gracefully on the ledge, projecting a holographic message:

"To the creators of NeoMural,

The world is watching, and it waits in eager anticipation. May your journey inspire cities across the globe to weave their tales.

With admiration,

World Arts and Culture Council."

Aria's eyes widened. "The WACC! Liam, this is big. Really big."

Liam took a deep breath, feeling the weight and wonder of what they had embarked upon. "NeoVille's story is just beginning. And so is ours."

Part Two

Echoes of Recognition

CHAPTER ELEVEN

Global Gaze

The morning sun painted NeoVille in gold, but the city was already abuzz with a different kind of shimmer—excitement. Reports had come in that the NeoMural project, originally a local endeavor, had caught the attention of international media. Screens across the city flashed headlines like, "NeoVille's Audacious Artistic Undertaking" and "The Mural Heard Around the World."

Liam, previously accustomed to the quiet anonymity of his artistry, now found himself thrust into sudden prominence. Every tech blog, art critique show, and international news outlet wanted a piece of the story. And behind this massive wave of attention was Aria, who had strategically released snippets of the project to key influencers in the art and tech world.

In their shared studio, a space that once felt so vast, Liam and Aria were swarmed with interview requests, holographic conference calls, and an unending stream of notifications. Aria, ever the tech-savvy and strategic one, thrived amidst this digital whirlwind. Liam, however, felt a growing unease.

One evening, as the sun cast long shadows over the city, Aria found Liam on the rooftop, lost in thought. "It's overwhelming, isn't it?" she remarked, joining him.

Liam sighed, "I wanted NeoVille to see itself, to find unity. I never imagined the whole world would be watching."

Aria smiled gently, "But that's the beauty of it, isn't it? Our story resonates. NeoVille's canvas has become a mirror for cities and communities everywhere. They see themselves in our mural."

But with recognition came responsibility. The international community wasn't just interested; they had opinions, suggestions, and critiques. Some admired the perfect blend of tech and art, while others feared that the very essence of raw, unfiltered art was at stake.

Late into the night, Liam received a message on his AR device. It was from Luca Ramirez, a renowned artist he had always admired. The message read, "Your work with the NeoMural is revolutionary. But remember, with global eyes upon you, stay true to your vision. The world doesn't just need another mural; it needs NeoVille's heart."

CHAPTER TWELVE

The Symposium of Synthesis

In the heart of NeoVille, a grand convention center known as The Nexus was being prepared for the much-anticipated Global Art-Tech Symposium. The event, usually hosted by iconic cities like Paris, New York, or Tokyo, had chosen NeoVille as its destination this year, thanks largely to the buzz surrounding the NeoMural.

The Nexus was a masterpiece in itself – walls composed of liquid crystal allowed for ever-changing sceneries, floors were interactive touch panels, and the ceiling was a vast augmented reality dome. Artists, tech moguls, critics, and enthusiasts from around the world poured into the city, their arrival amplifying the anticipation that was already palpable in NeoVille's air.

Aria was in her element, networking with tech innovators, sharing her visions and absorbing theirs. The intersection of art and technology was evolving, and she was keen to ensure NeoVille remained at the forefront.

Liam, meanwhile, felt like a fish out of water. Amongst the elite, the connoisseurs of art, he often found himself second-guessing his instincts. Doubts whispered, "Was the NeoMural truly groundbreaking, or was it just a fleeting novelty?"

The highlight of the symposium was a panel discussion titled "Art in the Age of Augmentation." To Liam's surprise, he was invited as a speaker alongside art-tech giants. The session was an intense, passionate debate. Traditional artists argued that tech was diluting the essence of raw expression, while futurists believed that technology amplified the soul of art, giving it wings it never had.

Liam listened, taking in each perspective. When it was his turn, he started by projecting an image of the early sketches of the NeoMural. "This," he began, "was born from pain, hope, unity, and dreams. The tech didn't replace the emotion; it simply gave it a voice loud enough to echo. It allowed individual stories to become a collective saga."

The room, filled with a mixture of skepticism and intrigue, fell into a hushed silence. Here was an artist who tread the line between tradition and tomorrow.

Post-discussion, a renowned artist from Paris approached Liam, "Your mural, it reminds me of the tales our city walls whisper. Different medium, same soul. Perhaps, NeoVille and Paris can collaborate?"

The proposition was tantalizing. A blend of NeoVille's futuristic vision with the timeless charm of Paris. The seed of a new dream was planted.

CHAPTER THIRTEEN

Dual Dimensions

The collaborative idea between NeoVille and Paris, termed "Project Dual Dimensions," quickly gained momentum. Its essence was to bridge two worlds: NeoVille's ultramodern art-tech canvas and the historical, iconic street art of Paris. The aim was to create two murals, one in each city, that would digitally interact in real-time, unifying the cities and cultures.

Liam found himself in Paris, amidst cobbled streets, historic cafés, and walls that whispered centuries of stories. Here, he was to collaborate with Claudette, a legendary Parisian street artist known for her evocative murals.

As they strolled along the Seine, Claudette shared her apprehensions. "Technology can be cold, but" she mused, her fingers brushing an aged stone wall, "These walls have seen revolutions, love stories, and eras go by. How does one ensure that the warmth isn't lost in the digital cold?"

Liam admitted his own concerns from when the NeoMural first began. "The challenge," he said, "isn't to let tech dominate, but to make it a vessel, a carrier of our emotions."

Their first collaborative piece was on the famous Le Mur Oberkampf, a space in Paris dedicated to changing urban art. Claudette's design was a beautiful rendition of the Seine flowing through time, while Liam added augmented reality elements—boats that moved, seasons that changed, and shadows of history that danced.

Back in NeoVille, Aria coordinated the digital synchronization. When someone in Paris interacted with their mural, a corresponding effect appeared on NeoVille's counterpart piece, and vice versa. The Seine's water would ripple in NeoVille, while NeoVille's futuristic skyline would morph into historical Parisian landmarks on Le Mur Oberkampf.

The project was not without its hiccups. Technical glitches, differences in artistic vision, and occasional bouts of nostalgia and homesickness for Liam. Yet, amidst it all, a masterpiece was emerging.

One evening, as Liam and Claudette painted under the Parisian twilight, an elderly woman approached them. Tearfully, she shared how the mural's historical shadows had brought back memories of her late husband—they'd met during a revolution. "Your art," she whispered, "has bridged my past and my present."

That night, thousands of miles apart, both Liam and Aria realized the profound impact of their work. Art wasn't just about aesthetics; it was a bridge across time, space, and souls.

CHAPTER FOURTEEN

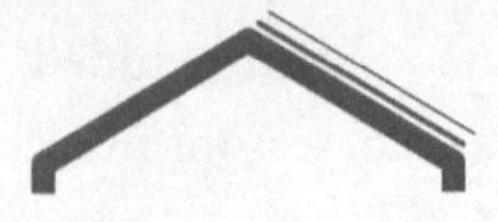

Pixels and Pretense

As "Project Dual Dimensions" advanced, both NeoVille and Paris became the cynosure for global art enthusiasts and socialites. NeoVille, especially, began to experience an influx of the world's elite, drawn like moths to the dazzling flame of the new-age mural magic.

The boulevards of NeoVille, previously frequented by genuine art lovers and curious locals, now also had a new breed of visitors—the 'Glamour Gazers'. This new crowd, with their high-end AR glasses, designer outfits, and a penchant for taking more selfies than absorbing the art, seemed more interested in being seen at the 'happening spot' than in the art itself.

Cafés that once echoed with profound discussions on artistry and technology now buzzed with chatter about which influencer was spotted where, and which tech mogul was investing in which startup. The essence of art was being overshadowed by the spectacle of social status.

Aria, ever the observer, found this evolution both amusing and disheartening. She began documenting it on her blog, penning down satirical pieces like "10 Ways to Pretend You Understand Art" and "The Guide to Looking Profound While Being Clueless." Her witty observations garnered laughter, but also ignited discussions on the dilution of art appreciation in the age of social media stardom.

Liam, in Paris, was initially oblivious to this cultural shift. But during a virtual meeting with Aria, he got a glimpse of the changing scene. He spotted a famous socialite, more known for her scandalous affairs than her love for art, posing dramatically in front of a piece of the NeoMural. "Is that...?" he began, only for Aria to chuckle, "Yes, and she apparently is an 'art expert' now."

Back in Paris, Claudette too had stories. She shared tales of tourists who would come to historical art spots, with audio guides playing in their ears, nodding pretentiously while understanding little. "It's a global trend, my friend. The age of instant gratification has made connoisseurs out of everyone. Or so they believe," she quipped.

However, amidst the satire and the superficial, the genuine art lovers persisted. They would often be found in quiet corners, eyes closed, letting the art speak to them, transcending the noise of the Glamour Gazers.

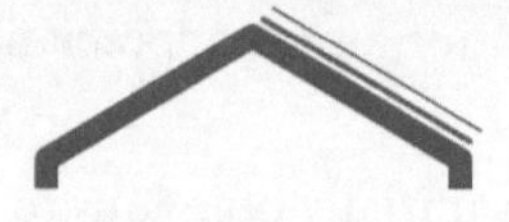

CHAPTER FIFTEEN

Virtual Virtues and Vices

With "Project Dual Dimensions" creating ripples in the international art scene, a new phase of tech integration began to emerge—Virtual Reality (VR) exhibitions. The idea was to allow people from any part of the world to virtually walk through the streets of Paris and NeoVille, experiencing the murals in all their interactive glory.

HyperTech, a leading tech company in NeoVille, approached Aria with a prototype VR headset. With these, users could not only see the murals but also feel the texture of the paint, the breeze of the environment, even the distant hum of the city.

Aria was captivated. This could democratize art access, breaking down geographical and economic barriers. A child in a remote village could now virtually stand in NeoVille or by the Seine in Paris, experiencing world-class art.

Yet, the VR exhibitions brought with them a set of challenges. As the boundary between reality and virtuality blurred, so did people's sense of presence. Many began to prefer the sanitized, controlled environment of the virtual world, devoid of real-world unpredictabilities like weather changes or street disturbances. NeoVille's streets, once bustling with visitors, started to see a decline as more people chose the comfort of their VR headsets.

Moreover, the sanctity of art was at stake. With VR, users could modify the murals to their liking, adding elements or erasing parts they didn't fancy. The NeoMural, a symbol of collective memory and unity, was at risk of becoming a canvas for individual whims.

Liam, during a call with Aria, voiced his concerns, "Art is meant to be felt with all our senses—the unpredictability of a breeze, the murmurs of onlookers, the imperfections. Do we lose that in a world that's too perfect?"

Aria, ever the tech optimist, countered, "But think of the reach, Liam. Think of those who can't travel or afford to come to NeoVille. For them, this is a window to a world they'd never see."

It was during one of these virtual exhibitions that a touching incident occurred. A message was relayed to Aria from a hospital in Brazil. A terminally ill child, bound to his bed, had virtually visited NeoVille. "For a few minutes," the message read, "he was a normal boy, walking through your city, eyes filled with wonder. Thank you."

This poignant moment made Aria and Liam realize the duality of progress. Every step forward brought benefits and challenges. The key was to strike a balance, ensuring that in the quest for universal access, the soul of art wasn't compromised.

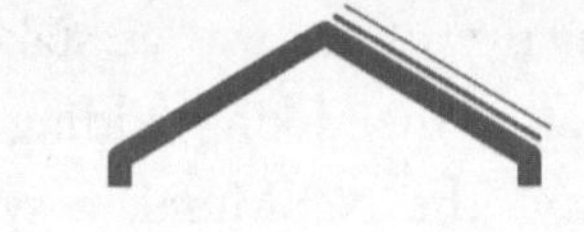

CHAPTER SIXTEEN

The Matrix of Morality

As weeks turned into months, the buzz surrounding the VR exhibitions and the NeoMural's digitization grew louder, eclipsing even the most famous landmarks of NeoVille. But as with any revolution, there were detractors. A particular group, calling themselves 'Realists,' began to challenge the integrity of this virtual experience.

"They are not just altering perspectives; they're altering reality!" decried Sarah Lenton, the outspoken leader of the Realists, during a virtual debate with Aria. "Art, at its core, should be a representation of the artist's truth, not a mutable plaything for the masses."

But it wasn't just the ideological arguments that became a point of contention. The economic implications were vast. Brick-and-mortar art galleries, which had been experiencing a decline, were now almost on the brink of extinction. Travel agencies that once flourished by arranging art tours felt the pinch. Local businesses in NeoVille, once benefiting from tourists, now saw dwindling footfalls as people preferred to "visit" from the comfort of their homes.

One evening, Liam, who had grown distant since the virtual boom, finally called Aria. "Aria," he began, voice laced with a weariness she hadn't heard before, "I've been offered a spot at a conventional art exhibition in New York. They want me to recreate the NeoMural, in its original form, without the digital layers."

Aria was silent. She remembered the joy and unity the original NeoMural had brought. "Would you do it?" she asked hesitantly.

"I want to," Liam replied, "I miss the tangibility, the rawness of real paint and real reactions."

Aria realized the emotional and moral conundrum they were in. The very technology that had given wings to their art now threatened to cage it. She missed the real-world reactions, the animated discussions among viewers, the look of awe in a child's eyes.

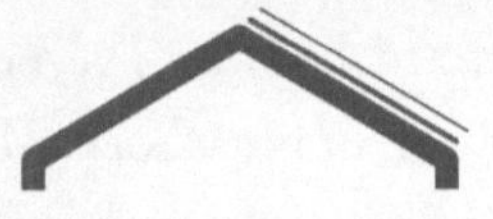

CHAPTER SEVENTEEN

Blurring Boundaries: Reality vs. Virtuality

The day of the traditional art exhibition in New York had arrived. Liam, with a flurry of brushes and a vivid palette of colors, recreated the NeoMural with a fervor Aria hadn't seen in months. She watched, torn between the allure of the tactile world of paints and canvases and the groundbreaking realm they'd ventured into with the digitized version.

During the creative storm, they reconnected. They reminisced about their journey, the highs, the lows, the revolution they had been part of, and the unintended ripples it had created. Liam, with a mischievous twinkle in his eyes, added a new element to the mural — a digital QR code. It wasn't just decorative; when scanned, it directed the viewer to the virtual NeoMural.

The juxtaposition was uncanny. Here was a traditional canvas with a portal to its virtual counterpart, a bridge between two worlds, challenging visitors to question their perceptions of reality.

Opening day saw an overwhelming turnout. Art enthusiasts, technophobes, tech gurus, and curious onlookers thronged the gallery. Aria observed a middle-aged woman, teary-eyed as she looked at the mural, being comforted by a young girl, probably her granddaughter. They then scanned the QR code together, venturing into the virtual realm hand-in-hand. Such scenes abounded, with multiple generations experiencing art in their preferred formats yet finding a common ground.

But the event was not without controversy. Sarah Lenton, ever the vocal critic, led a protest outside. "Preserve Real Art," read one sign. "Virtual is Not Reality," declared another. However, even some Realists were seen sneaking curious glances, and a few bravely ventured inside, immersing themselves in the dual experience.

Liam approached Sarah, trying to bridge the divide. "Art evolves, just as we do," he said calmly. "This isn't about replacing, but augmenting. Let's find a way to make this work."

CHAPTER EIGHTEEN

The Dissonance of Digital Dominion

The success of the New York exhibition reverberated through the art world. Liam and Aria's dual-format exhibition became a topic of global discussion, stirring both admiration and dissent. The digitization wave had grown exponentially, sweeping through various art forms. It wasn't just murals; sculptures, classical paintings, and even performance arts had been given a digital twist.

With the rise of digital art came a plethora of opportunities, but also complications. The boundary between the creator and the audience began to blur, as more people could modify and adapt artworks in virtual realms. An artist might create a sculpture in one vision, only for it to be altered and reshared, oftentimes without due credit.

NeoVille, as the birthplace of the digital art revolution, found itself at the forefront of these challenges. Digital art classes flourished, and young artists stormed the virtual realm with their interpretations. But the questions loomed: Where does artistic freedom end, and where does appropriation begin? How does one protect the sanctity of the original creation?

Liam and Aria, having tasted both sides of the coin, were at an impasse. Aria, ever the innovator, believed in fluidity and the organic evolution of art. "Art is a conversation," she would often say, "and conversations evolve."

Liam, having reconnected with the tangible texture of paint and canvas, felt an increasing need to safeguard artists' rights. "There's a fine line between inspiration and imitation," he countered.

A pivotal scene unfolded at NeoVille's Digital Art Symposium. As Aria showcased the endless possibilities of digital alterations, emphasizing co-creation, Liam unveiled a prototype of a digital watermark – a dynamic signature that morphed and adjusted as art was altered, ensuring the original artist was always credited.

Sarah Lenton, surprisingly, voiced her support for Liam's innovation. "While I may not fully embrace this digital era," she confessed, "I respect the need for artistic integrity. And this," she pointed to the watermark, "is a step in the right direction."

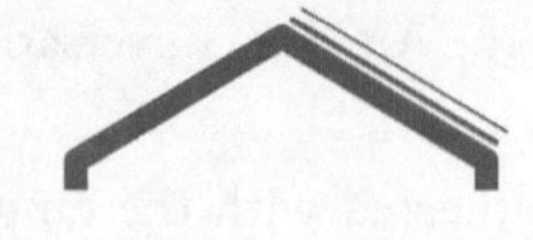

CHAPTER NINETEEN

Unity in Unpredictability

News of the digital watermark spread rapidly. It wasn't just the art world that took notice; tech companies and digital innovators were keen to understand and integrate Liam's groundbreaking creation. The watermark, however, was still in its prototype phase, and Liam was inundated with collaboration offers and requests for demonstrations.

Amidst this whirlwind, a curious invitation arrived: The Global Art-Tech Fusion Summit in Tokyo. This annual event was renowned for being the melting pot of art and technology, and this year's theme was "Blended Realities."

Aria, feeling a tad alienated with the sudden shift towards preservation over innovation, was hesitant to attend. But the promise of new technological wonders and the potential to mold the future of digital art proved too enticing to resist.

Tokyo was a city of contrasts – ancient temples nestled among towering skyscrapers, serene gardens juxtaposed against bustling tech hubs. It was here that Aria had an epiphany. Watching a traditional tea ceremony, she marveled at the meticulous attention to detail and realized that, much like the tea being brewed, the essence of art was in its authenticity, regardless of the medium.

At the summit, while Liam showcased the watermark's capabilities, Aria presented an intriguing concept: "Echo Chambers of Creation." She proposed dedicated virtual realms where artists could collaboratively create, uninhibited by the constraints of copyrights, yet with the acknowledgment that these were spaces of free expression and anything birthed here was for the collective. A true Utopia for the artists, by the artists.

The proposal was met with thunderous applause. Many saw it as a compromise between the unfettered freedom of digital art and the respect for individual creativity.

As the summit progressed, unexpected alliances were forged. Traditional artisans collaborated with VR experts to craft experiences that were both authentic and futuristic. A renowned sculptor paired up with a holography whiz to create floating, evolving sculptures.

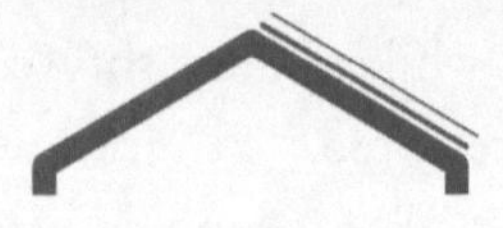

CHAPTER TWENTY

Synthesis at Sunrise

Post-summit, Tokyo transformed from a bustling metropolis to a serene haven for Liam and Aria. They decided to extend their stay, soaking in the cultural nuances and technological advancements that the city seamlessly wove together.

One early morning, as the first rays of sunlight painted the city in hues of gold, they found themselves atop the Tokyo Skytree, overlooking the sprawling cityscape. It was here, amidst the quietude of dawn, that they reflected on their tumultuous journey.

"I used to believe that to move forward, we had to let go of the past," Aria murmured, watching the horizon. "But now, I see the beauty in amalgamation. The past doesn't weigh us down; it anchors us, giving meaning to our flight."

Liam smiled, taking her hand. "Our journey, our disagreements, they were necessary. They were the friction that sparked this new path. We've laid the groundwork for something truly transcendent."

Below them, Tokyo was waking up. Traditional markets setting up for the day's trade were interspersed with neon billboards advertising the latest VR tech. The harmonious coexistence of history and future was palpable.

Inspired, they began sketching out plans for a new venture: An Art-Tech Fusion Lab in NeoVille. A space that would not only champion innovations like the digital watermark but also serve as a sanctuary for traditional art forms, ensuring they were not lost in the digital deluge.

News of their initiative spread, and by the time they returned to NeoVille, the community was abuzz with anticipation. The ground-breaking ceremony of the Fusion Lab was a grand affair, attended by residents, artists, tech moguls, and even Sarah Lenton, who had begun to soften her stance.

The act culminated with Aria and Liam unveiling a collaborative piece – a tangible mural that seamlessly transitioned into a digital realm when viewed through special lenses. It was a celebration of their journey, a tapestry of trials, triumphs, and the promise of a harmonious future.

As attendees marveled at the masterpiece, the scene faded with the setting sun, mirroring the sunrise in Tokyo, signaling an end yet hinting at new beginnings.

Part Three

Reverberations of Reality

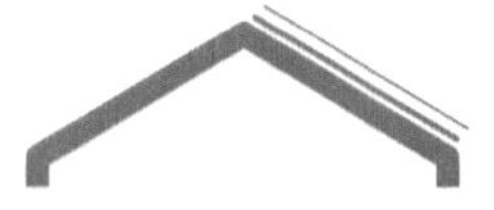

CHAPTER TWENTY-ONE

Quest for Quiescence

The NeoVille nightscape, usually a vibrant play of neon and shadow, was noticeably subdued. The glowing billboards and interactive advertisements appeared a touch less bright, reflecting the somber mood of the town's artistic community. The Fusion Lab's incident had become the talk of the town, dominating dinner table discussions and digital forums alike.

Aria, usually so attuned to NeoVille's rhythm, felt out of sync. The clamor of accusations and defenses, the urgent whisperings in corridors, and the quiet tears of artisans fearing the loss of their legacy weighed heavily on her. Each evening, she found herself drawn to NeoVille's outskirts, seeking solace in the old forests that bordered the town — a place where the cacophony of the present was muffled by the enduring whispers of ancient trees.

It was during one such twilight walk that Aria stumbled upon an old, decrepit chapel. The stained-glass windows, although dusty, threw patterns on the floor, reminiscent of the mosaic at Fusion Lab. Inside, it was cool and silent, save for the distant hoot of an owl.

Finding a pew, Aria let out a sigh. The silence wasn't just the absence of noise; it was palpable, comforting, almost as if the chapel was absorbing all her anxieties, giving her a blank slate.

As minutes turned to hours, a thought began forming in Aria's mind. Perhaps, what the Fusion Lab needed was not more dialogue, but a moment of collective silence. A space and time where artists could reconnect with their inner muse, away from the clamor of egos and ideologies. A reset of sorts.

She left the chapel with a budding plan. She'd invite artists from both factions for a silent retreat. No discussions, no debates—just them and their art, immersed in NeoVille's natural beauty.

On her way back, the city lights seemed a touch brighter, the billboards more colorful. Maybe, just maybe, in seeking quiescence, they'd find the answers that eluded them in the noise.

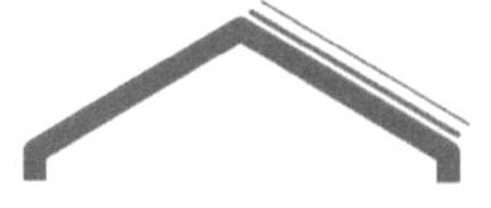

CHAPTER TWENTY-TWO

Navigating Neo-Normal

The idea of a silent retreat spread like wildfire across the Fusion Lab's grapevine. Surprisingly, many artists were intrigued, yearning for an escape from the heated ambiance that had become the Lab's neo-normal.

Liam, who initially raised an eyebrow at Aria's idea, quickly came around. "Sometimes, I feel technology itself yearns for a break," he quipped, fingers gliding over his latest creation, a 4D sketch pad.

As the day of the retreat neared, Aria found herself at the helm of a logistical challenge. The traditionalists wanted natural canvases, tools, and paints, while the technophiles wished for their gadgets charged and ready. Striking a balance, Aria decided to limit the number of tech devices and ensured all tools harmoniously integrated with the environment.

The retreat site, set amidst the NeoVille forest, was a blend of the old and new. Tents, made from biodegradable materials, boasted holographic displays. Campfires, fueled by eco-pellets, also served as wireless charging points. The very design seemed to whisper the possibility of coexistence.

On the inaugural evening, artists sat around the campfire, the flickering flames casting silhouettes on their faces. The only sound was the rustling of leaves, the distant chirp of night creatures, and the soft hum of tech devices.

Sarah Lenton, still seething from the mural incident, found herself sketching on a digital tablet, lent by a young tech artist named Jonah. While she missed the tactile feel of brush and canvas, the sheer range of colors and textures the tablet offered was mesmerizing.

Jonah, in turn, was engrossed in a hand-carved wooden sculpture, his fingers relishing the grainy texture of the wood, marveling at its tangible realness.

As days melted into nights, artists discovered new mediums and techniques, often guided by their supposed 'adversaries.' The retreat wasn't devoid of disagreements, but the absence of verbal arguments led to more expressions through art. An intricate mural began taking shape on a large canvas, a collaboration of pixels and paint, embodying the essence of the Fusion Lab.

When the retreat ended, the artists returned, not to the old Fusion Lab, but a transformed space. The 'neo-normal' wasn't about choosing sides but cherishing the shared canvas of creativity.

CHAPTER TWENTY-THREE

Harmony and Holographs

Back at the Fusion Lab, a renewed energy permeated the atmosphere. While the memory of the disputes remained, they seemed like remnants of a bygone era, relegated to the background amidst the newfound harmony.

One of the most poignant outcomes of the retreat was the realization that while technology and tradition might speak different languages, their narratives converged on the universal canvas of creativity. The artists began to view their counterparts not as competition but as complements.

Jonah, the young digital maestro, and Sarah, the guardian of tradition, became the unexpected flagbearers of this change. They embarked on a project that epitomized the Lab's ethos: a living, breathing holographic mural.

On a massive expanse of wall, Sarah started with broad strokes of deep blues and ethereal greens, depicting a tranquil night sky. She poured her emotions onto the canvas, letting the colors narrate tales of the ancients.

Adjacent to her, Jonah's holograph device whirred to life. It captured the hues and intricacies of Sarah's painting and extended them into the third dimension. An eagle painted by Sarah suddenly soared out of the canvas, its holographic counterpart gliding gracefully above the awestruck onlookers. The line between the physical and digital world seemed to blur, creating a surreal dreamscape.

It wasn't just Sarah and Jonah. Everywhere one looked, collaborative ventures bloomed. A sculptor molded clay, only for a tech artist to encase it in a shimmering digital aurora. A pianist's tune became the background score for a virtual reality experience, allowing users to 'walk' through a painted landscape.

The most enchanting aspect of this transformation was the nightly showcase. The Fusion Lab's facade would come alive with projections of the day's collaborative pieces. Traditional motifs danced seamlessly with futuristic designs, drawing residents and tourists alike, all entranced by the magical confluence.

Yet, while the Fusion Lab buzzed with activity, Aria and Liam often found themselves retreating to their quiet corner, reminiscing about their journey. They had learned that harmony wasn't a destination but an ongoing process, and they were just getting started.

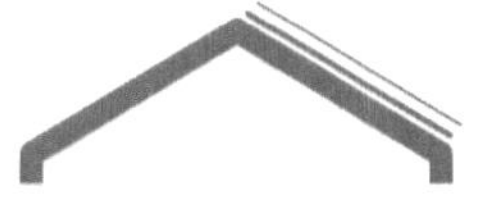

CHAPTER TWENTY-FOUR

Dystopia's Dawn

Despite the harmony within the Fusion Lab, the world outside its walls was in flux. NeoVille, for all its futuristic allure, was beginning to show cracks in its façade. The relentless pursuit of innovation had led to disparities in wealth and accessibility. The city's underbelly, ignored for so long, was now becoming a pulsating sore.

As Aria and Liam ventured out one day to source materials, they stumbled upon a part of NeoVille they had rarely seen before. Far from the glitzy skyscrapers and neon billboards lay dilapidated huts, children playing with discarded tech parts, and elders narrating tales of a time when life was simpler.

Here, the reverberations of reality were stark. People were either clinging desperately to the remnants of the past or scavenging the throwaways of the futuristic elite. There was no fusion, no collaboration—only a chasm.

A young girl, no older than twelve, approached Aria with a handmade bracelet. It was crafted with care, using both colorful threads and salvaged microchips. In her eyes, Aria saw a spark—a yearning for a bridge between her world and the dazzling heights of NeoVille.

The experience was a sobering reminder for both Aria and Liam. The Fusion Lab, with its melding of tradition and technology, was but a bubble in a city divided. Their vision needed to extend beyond the Lab's walls.

Driven by this realization, they initiated a program called "Echoes of Unity." This program would invite the residents of NeoVille's forgotten corners to collaborate with the Fusion Lab's artists. Workshops were designed to teach traditional crafts to the tech-savvy and introduce the magic of technology to artisans.

But, not everyone was pleased. The Lab faced criticism from sections of NeoVille's elite, who viewed this as a dilution of their progressive city's essence. There were hurdles, both logistical and ideological. However, Aria and Liam persisted, believing in the power of unity.

As weeks turned into months, a transformation began to unfold. The Fusion Lab's nightly showcases began to attract diverse audiences. The tales told on the facade were no longer just of artistic harmony but of a city finding its soul.

In "Dystopia's Dawn," the narrative reminds readers that while pockets of harmony are beautiful, true progress is achieved when an entire society finds its rhythm, and no echo, no matter how faint, is left unheard.

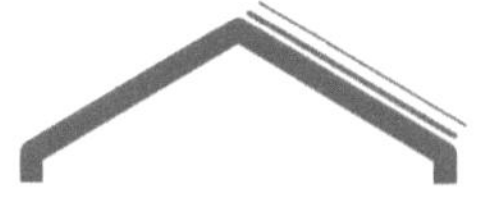

CHAPTER TWENTY-FIVE

Awakening Amidst Anomalies

The Fusion Lab's 'Echoes of Unity' initiative was beginning to resonate throughout NeoVille. Every street corner seemed to be reverberating with collaborative art. From holographic plays reimagining ancient legends, to elderly folk guiding young techies in crafting intricate wearable tech based on age-old designs, the city seemed to be in the throes of a cultural renaissance.

Yet, anomalies began to emerge, subtle at first, but increasingly noticeable.

Liam first caught onto it during a demonstration of his newest invention, a device that captured an artist's emotional state and translated it into visual art. But, during a public presentation, the device began projecting erratic, dystopian images, even when the artist was evidently at peace. Whispers of technological malfunctions rippled across the audience.

Similarly, Aria, while mentoring a group on classic mural painting, noticed unusual patterns appearing on her canvas—ones she hadn't painted. They resembled circuitry layouts, intertwined with her traditional patterns, creating an unintentional, chaotic blend.

Across NeoVille, technology seemed to be misbehaving. Self-driving vehicles took unexpected detours, singing fountains played dissonant notes, and digital billboards glitched, showcasing a blend of advertisements from decades gone by.

Rumors began to swirl. Some believed the city's AI was gaining sentience, rebelling against its creators. Others argued that NeoVille's rapid expansion and fusion experiments were causing technological rifts.

Aria and Liam found themselves at the epicenter, trying to decipher these anomalies. They realized that the very essence of their work—blending the past with the future—might be key to understanding what was happening.

Delving deep, they discovered that the city's foundational tech was based on algorithms inspired by ancient patterns and rhythms. The current blending of tradition and technology wasn't just a superficial overlay but resonated with the core code of NeoVille.

A breakthrough came when they collaborated with the city's oldest inhabitants and its brightest tech minds. These anomalies were not rebellions but awakenings. The city's tech was resonating with the newfound unity, trying to recalibrate and find its own harmony.

The solution lay in embracing, not resisting. Instead of trying to 'fix' the anomalies, residents were encouraged to interact with them, integrate them, and understand them. Slowly, the dystopian images became art pieces, the erratic vehicle paths became scenic routes, and the city's glitches transformed into attractions.

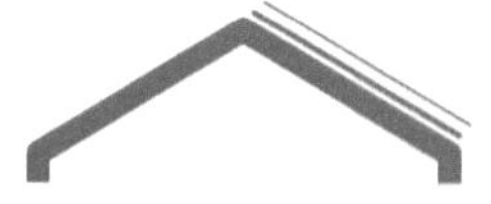

CHAPTER TWENTY-SIX

Legacy of the Lost

Amid the technological riddles and the bustling renaissance, a quieter, subtler undercurrent was unfolding. Elderly residents of NeoVille began to share tales from before the city's rise to futuristic prominence. These were stories lost in the rush towards innovation, tales of traditions, rituals, and customs that had shaped the old world.

An old man named Elias became the unlikely torchbearer of this movement. He had lived through the transition from the old world to NeoVille and had seen the city's ancestors live harmoniously with nature. To the younger generation, he often spoke of "The Time of Tenderness" – an era where people and the planet were partners, not competitors.

Intrigued by these tales, Aria and Liam decided to document this oral history. They initiated "Project Legacy", an endeavor that would use the latest holographic tech to bring these tales to life. The idea was to create a virtual library where NeoVillians could walk through the stories of the past and experience them firsthand.

As Elias and others narrated their memories, the technology painted vivid, immersive landscapes. Visitors could feel the cool shade of trees now extinct, hear the calls of birds long gone, and see the rituals that once marked the passage of seasons.

However, this wasn't mere nostalgia. As more and more people visited the library, a realization began to dawn. NeoVille, in its quest for the future, had inadvertently left behind invaluable wisdom. The city's current challenges – from technological anomalies to social divides – had, in some form, been faced and addressed by their ancestors. The old ways offered insights, not just about where they came from, but where they should be headed.

A particularly poignant moment occurred when a young tech prodigy, after a virtual walk through "The Time of Tenderness", redesigned a major city transport route to reincorporate a river which had been buried under concrete. The river's reintroduction not only solved water scarcity issues but also rejuvenated community spaces.

"Project Legacy" started as a tribute but soon became a guidepost. NeoVille began to understand that their ancestors' legacy wasn't an anchor to the past but a compass for the future.

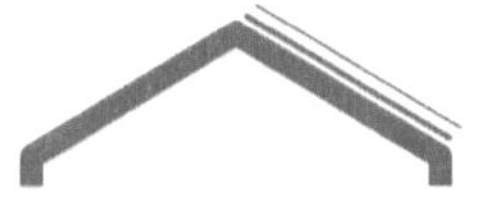

CHAPTER TWENTY-SEVEN

Reconciliation and Resurgence

The anomalies of NeoVille, although initially disruptive, had inadvertently fostered an environment ripe for introspection. The city, which had for so long raced towards the future, was now pausing, reflecting, and connecting with its roots.

"Project Legacy" was the catalyst that spurred many to revisit the forgotten sections of NeoVille. The tech elites, who once scoffed at the notions of tradition, began frequenting the quarters where tech and tradition seamlessly fused. The old and the young started communicating more, exchanging wisdom for innovation and vice versa.

Aria and Liam, after the success of their initiative, became unofficial ambassadors for bridging divides. Their next venture aimed to resolve a longstanding issue in NeoVille: the segregation between the creators and the consumers, the artists and the audience, the techies and the traditionalists.

Labelled "The Confluence Project", it was an ambitious plan to redesign public spaces in NeoVille. Instead of having separate zones for art, tech demonstrations, relaxation, and trade, they proposed integrated zones where all these activities could intermingle.

At the heart of each zone was a 'Confluence Circle' – an interactive platform where an artist could create, a techie could demo, and the audience could participate, all in real-time. The circle's tech would respond to the emotions and reactions of the crowd, adjusting the experience in real-time. It was a stage, a lab, and a canvas, all in one.

The results were electric. A dance performance would be enhanced with holographic histories of the dance form, tech demos became art pieces with historical context, and traditional craft markets showcased futuristic applications of their goods.

The true highlight was when Elias, the torchbearer of old tales, stood at a Confluence Circle. As he narrated stories, the audience, using their personal tech, contributed visuals, sounds, and sensory elements. It became a collaborative storytelling experience, a dance of the past and the future, and a testament to NeoVille's newfound unity.

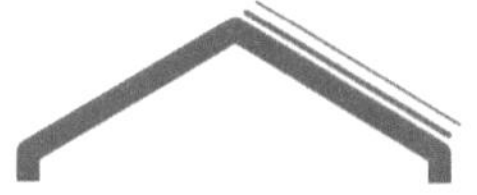

CHAPTER TWENTY-EIGHT

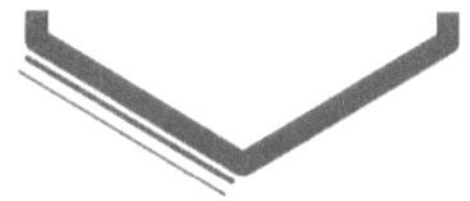

Endearing Echoes: The NeoMural's Nexus

The momentum of unity and integration in NeoVille had reached a fervent pace, and everyone was keen on immortalizing this era of transformation. The proposal? A monumental mural, representing the city's journey, from its inception to its present day. The mural would not be painted on a traditional canvas, but rather on a massive holographic screen that spanned the central plaza, ensuring that it was visible from any corner of NeoVille.

The NeoMural, as it came to be known, was no ordinary project. Aria and Liam envisioned it as a dynamic artwork that would evolve in real-time, responding to the narratives, emotions, and innovations of the city.

To ensure everyone's voice was heard, they set up numerous Confluence Circles at various points in the city. Here, residents could share stories, memories, dreams, and hopes. The data would be collected, and an advanced AI, combined with artistic direction, would convert these stories into visual elements for the NeoMural.

Elias, with his treasure trove of tales, was given a prominent Confluence Circle. Yet, it was the young, the dreamers, the innovators, and even the skeptics who flocked to share, contributing in vibrant ways. Each had a distinct voice, a unique perspective. There were tales of ambition, tales of loss, hopes for the future, and echoes of the past.

As the days turned into nights and weeks melted into months, the NeoMural began to take shape. At first glance, it looked chaotic, with hues of every color, forms of every kind intertwining, and narratives crisscrossing. But as one looked deeper, patterns emerged. The beauty was in the details, in the juxtaposition, in the contradictions and harmonies.

The city's skyline, its historical landmarks, its tech marvels, and its people—every element was depicted. Yet, they weren't stagnant. They morphed and changed, reflecting the dynamic nature of NeoVille. The mural showcased not just a city, but a living entity.

The unveiling was a citywide celebration. NeoVille's heart seemed to beat in sync with the NeoMural's shimmering glow. Aria, Liam, Elias, and countless others watched, mesmerized. It was a testament to their journey, a reflection of their unity, and a beacon for their future.

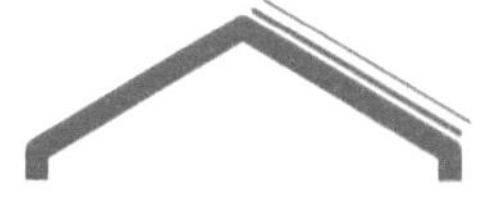

CHAPTER TWENTY-NINE

Tomorrow's Tapestry: The Ties That Bind

With the NeoMural shining as the living, breathing heart of NeoVille, the spirit of the city was palpable. However, Aria and Liam, ever the visionaries, believed there was more to be done. They wished for the sentiment behind the mural—a unified and harmonious city—to permeate every aspect of NeoVille life, not just remain a visual testament.

The idea for "Tomorrow's Tapestry" was birthed from this very thought. It wasn't to be a physical object, but a community-driven initiative to weave the values, lessons, and stories from the NeoMural into the city's daily life.

Education was the starting point. Schools began including modules that used augmented reality to dive into the NeoMural. Children could interact with key events, figures, and innovations from NeoVille's history, understanding the context and the evolution of their society.

The corporate sector wasn't far behind. Workspaces integrated 'Legacy Hours' into their schedules, where employees engaged in group discussions, workshops, and team projects that drew inspiration from the mural. They tackled current challenges using the wisdom of the past and the innovations of the present, fostering a work culture rooted in collaboration and continuity.

But the most heartwarming implementation was in the residential districts. Communities began organizing "Tapestry Talks" – weekly gatherings where residents came together, much like the Confluence Circles, to share, discuss, and dream. The gatherings became melting pots of ideas, with elders and youngsters, techies and traditionalists, all sharing their perspectives.

As months passed, NeoVille began to transform. It wasn't just about the tangible improvements—although there were many, from sustainable tech solutions to community-driven welfare initiatives. It was the intangibles that truly stood out. Trust flourished. Empathy became the norm. People valued stories, experiences, and the shared journey of their city.

By the end of the chapter, NeoVille wasn't just a city; it was an intricate tapestry, each thread representing a citizen, their dreams, their struggles, and their hopes. And as every tapestry does, it provided warmth, comfort, and a sense of belonging.

CHAPTER THIRTY

Renaissance: The Resounding Reverie

In the heart of NeoVille, with the NeoMural's vibrant hues playing across its skies and the hum of a city united in purpose, an air of anticipation was palpable. The efforts of Aria, Liam, Elias, and countless others had woven a narrative of unity, innovation, and introspection.

However, as with all tales, there remained challenges yet to be tackled and stories yet to be told. NeoVille, now at the pinnacle of its Renaissance, stood at the precipice of another significant shift. The community-driven initiatives had made an undeniable impact, but whispers of a broader horizon beckoned.

Elias, with a glint in his eyes, spoke one day at a Tapestry Talk. "The NeoMural, the Confluence Circles, the Tomorrow's Tapestry initiative... they've all brought us closer as a community. But NeoVille isn't an isolated entity. What if we expanded our horizons, connected with communities beyond our boundaries, and started a global dialogue?"

This idea resonated deeply with Aria and Liam. The duo realized that while NeoVille had managed to find its harmony, the world outside still grappled with discord, disparity, and disconnect. If the methods and models developed in NeoVille could be adapted and shared, a global renaissance was possible.

A global consortium was envisioned – a platform where cities worldwide could come together, share their stories, challenges, and innovations. NeoVille would be the pilot, the guiding light, but every city would have its unique voice.

The chapter culminates with a grand event – the "Reverie Symposium" – where representatives from various global communities are invited to NeoVille. They're taken on a journey through the city, experiencing firsthand the magic of the NeoMural, the wisdom exchanges at the Tapestry Talks, and the collaborative ethos of the Confluence Circles.

The event ends with an impassioned speech by Liam. "NeoVille found its song, its rhythm in the echoes of yesterday and the promise of tomorrow. It's now time to help the world find its symphony."

As the representatives leave, they carry with them not just memories of a city reborn, but blueprints, ideas, and most importantly, hope.

Part Four

Synergy of the Spheres

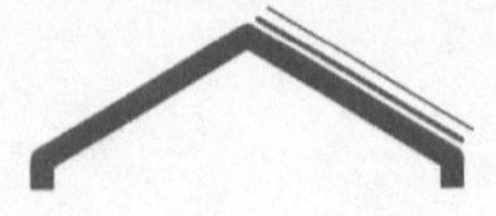

CHAPTER THIRTY-ONE

Intercontinental Inspirations

Aria stood at the panoramic windows of NeoVille's tallest skyscraper, NeoNest. The city stretched beneath her like a glimmering blanket, its lights a testament to its thriving night life and relentless pursuit of progress. She remembered the days when most of these lights were but a distant dream, and the city was a gray landscape of unfulfilled aspirations.

Her thoughts were interrupted by a ping from her digital pad. A news notification highlighted headlines from around the world. She glanced briefly, eyes pausing on a story about a town in Africa integrating virtual art into its educational system, similar to NeoVille's approach. Another mentioned a city in Europe adopting a sustainable model inspired by NeoVille's renewable energy initiatives.

Liam walked up beside her, two cups of synthesized coffee in hand. "Seen this?" he motioned to his own digital pad, displaying an article on a South American city developing a digital district modeled after NeoVille.

She smiled, "The world's catching on."

Liam took a sip, looking out into the skyline. "It's incredible to think about, isn't it? We dreamed of creating something monumental for NeoVille, but we never imagined our story would inspire entire cities."

Aria replied, "It's synergy, Liam. The beauty of shared ideas and collective progress. We provided a spark, and now it's catching fire everywhere."

Their reverie was interrupted by the entrance of Mayor Elara, who had been a consistent pillar of support throughout NeoVille's transformation. "I've been receiving invitations from cities globally," she began, her voice hinting at her excitement. "They want us to share NeoVille's blueprint. They want to collaborate, to adapt our models to their unique challenges."

Liam looked intrigued, "Intercontinental collaborations?"

Elara nodded, "It's time for NeoVille to step onto the global stage. Not just as an inspiration, but as a partner."

Aria mused, "A global network of cities, each learning from the other, each contributing to the collective story of progress."

The possibilities seemed endless. The synergy they had achieved within NeoVille had the potential to expand, enveloping continents, cultures, and communities. As NeoVille's achievements echoed across oceans, so too did its responsibility to share, learn, and grow.

The trio sat, brainstorming how best to begin this new chapter. NeoVille's local success story was poised to become an intercontinental inspiration, the first verse of a global anthem of progress and unity. The journey ahead was vast, but the promise of a united global community, working hand in hand, made the horizon seem tantalizingly close. The age of isolated progress was over; the era of synergy had begun.

CHAPTER THIRTY-TWO

Digital Diplomacy

NeoVille's town hall had always been an emblem of decision-making and traditional governance. But today, it took on a modern twist, buzzing with energy as technocrats, city planners, and innovative minds congregated. The purpose was clear: to ideate a platform allowing cities globally to collaborate seamlessly.

Elara began the discussion, her enthusiasm evident, "Our goal isn't just to share NeoVille's blueprint, but to create a dialogue where cities can exchange their experiences, challenges, and solutions. NeoVille will be a contributor, but not the only voice."

A tech-savvy member from NeoVille's development team pitched in, "Imagine a digital forum, like a 'United Nations of Cities'. A place where representatives from cities worldwide can virtually meet, share, and collaborate in real-time."

Liam, always the visionary, took it a step further, "Not just discussion boards, but virtual reality spaces. Real-time simulations where city planners can walk through digital renditions of projects, test out infrastructure changes, even visualize the impact of policies before they're implemented."

The room buzzed with excitement. Aria, engrossed in thought, sketched a blueprint on her digital pad. "Cities can have profiles detailing their demographics, infrastructure, cultural elements, and innovations. These profiles can then be matched with challenges and solutions from other cities. It's like pairing problems with proven solutions, tailored to fit."

A young coder voiced a pertinent concern, "But how do we ensure equitable representation? We don't want this platform to become an echo chamber for only the most advanced cities."

Elara nodded in agreement, "Inclusivity will be our guiding principle. We'll have to ensure even the smallest towns have the tools and knowledge to contribute and benefit. Every city, no matter its size or resources, has something invaluable to share."

Liam added, "Perhaps we can integrate an AI-driven translator, ensuring language isn't a barrier. And maybe, just maybe, we can incorporate a cultural sensitivity module, ensuring interactions respect and honor local traditions and customs."

Aria smiled, thinking of their global aspirations. "Digital Diplomacy," she murmured. The term resonated with everyone, encapsulating their vision perfectly.

Weeks turned into months as the idea transformed into 'CityNet'. The platform was sophisticated yet user-friendly. News spread, and cities from all corners of the world began creating profiles. From Tokyo's efficient urban transport methods to Nairobi's sustainable agricultural innovations, CityNet became a digital repository of human progress.

In the heart of NeoVille, a new landmark rose, the CityNet Hub, a place where any citizen could walk in and explore global city innovations through immersive virtual reality.

The Digital Diplomacy initiative had truly begun, transforming isolated pockets of progress into an interwoven tapestry of global innovation. And at its core was the belief that by sharing and collaborating, the world's cities could create a brighter, unified future for all their inhabitants.

CHAPTER THIRTY-THREE

Patterns of Progress

The shimmering lights of NeoVille had always inspired awe, but now they took on a new meaning. Each pulsing hue seemed to represent a connection to a distant city, each flashing pattern indicative of shared knowledge, weaving an intricate global network of interconnectedness.

A few months post the launch of CityNet, stories of transformative change began pouring in. A small town in India adopted Seoul's waste management strategies, resulting in a cleaner environment for its residents. Amsterdam's canal revitalization techniques inspired coastal cities in Africa, fostering both tourism and aquatic life. The digital conversations were rapidly translating into tangible progress.

Liam was conducting a weekly review session in the CityNet Hub, showcasing some of the most inspiring stories. "There's a pattern," he started, flicking through visuals on the massive display screen. "It's not just about cities adopting technological advancements. It's about them recognizing and adapting innovations to their cultural and socio-economic fabric. It's holistic progress."

Aria nodded, her eyes fixed on an animated graph. "It's fascinating to see. Here's a town in Argentina that's merged

Japanese Zen garden principles with local art to create public relaxation spaces. And look at this," she pointed to another visual, "A Canadian city is borrowing urban farming techniques from Vietnam, ensuring food security for its residents."

Elara, ever the proud mayor, chimed in, "What's more heartening is that NeoVille's digital art revolution is becoming a beacon of hope for cities devastated by natural calamities. They're using digital murals to rebuild, rejuvenate, and inspire resilience. We've started something beyond our wildest imaginations."

Liam leaned forward, his gaze intense. "While these stories are inspiring, it's essential we also focus on the challenges. Some cities still struggle to translate this shared knowledge into action due to infrastructural or political constraints."

A young data analyst, Clara, spoke up, her voice filled with conviction, "That's the beauty of patterns, Liam. They help predict. With the vast data we have, we can foresee which cities might face implementation challenges and proactively offer solutions or collaborations. Instead of just being reactive, CityNet can be a tool for predictive assistance."

The room went silent, processing Clara's insight. Aria broke the silence, her voice filled with determination, "Let's do it. Let's not just share success stories but also address challenges head-on. Let's ensure every city, every town, irrespective of its challenges, has its own pattern of progress."

As the days turned into nights, NeoVille continued to pulsate with energy, each light, each pattern, echoing stories of progress, challenges, resilience, and hope. It wasn't just about being a beacon anymore; it was about ensuring every light across the globe shone just as bright, every pattern as intricate and beautiful. The dance of interconnectedness had truly begun, and it was breathtaking.

CHAPTER THIRTY-FOUR

Echoing Enclaves

The sun had barely touched the horizon, painting the morning sky with hues of amber and rose, as Liam wandered the streets of NeoVille. He had often taken these early morning strolls, but today was different. The murmurs of change were palpable, almost tactile. Along the route, he stumbled upon 'Echoing Enclaves'—areas in the city that had been transformed into mini replicas of global towns.

The first enclave was a tribute to a picturesque town in Greece. Whitewashed buildings, blooming bougainvillea, and cozy tavernas serving aromatic Greek coffee filled the space. Residents chatted in the central plaza, sharing stories of their recent virtual trips via CityNet to the actual Grecian town. A holographic portal stood at the enclave's heart, providing real-time glimpses into the town's daily life.

Further ahead, an Italian piazza came to life. Authentic Neapolitan pizzas wafted through the air, as NeoVille's denizens enjoyed a virtual Venetian gondola ride or experienced the Roman Colosseum's majesty.

"What's remarkable," Aria commented, joining Liam in his walk, "is that these enclaves aren't just about aesthetic replications. They're about understanding the essence, the culture, and the struggles of these towns. They're about forging deep, empathetic connections."

Liam nodded, "It's not just about the beauty, but about the bonds. These spaces allow us to walk in their shoes, appreciate their achievements, and understand their challenges."

As they wandered, they reached an enclave echoing a town from Kenya. Mud huts juxtaposed with advanced digital interfaces showcased the blend of tradition and modernity. Locals demonstrated their artisanal crafts, while digital booths highlighted their progress in sustainable agriculture and wildlife conservation.

Elara, overseeing a new Moroccan enclave's inauguration, joined the conversation, "These Echoing Enclaves serve a dual purpose. While they deepen our global understanding, they also generate revenue. A part of the proceeds from each enclave is directed back to the original town, aiding in their developmental projects."

Aria smiled, looking at the children playing in the Kenyan enclave's simulation of the Maasai Mara, "These enclaves echo more than just appearances; they echo hopes, dreams, aspirations, and the undeniable proof that humanity, regardless of borders, shares a unified heart."

The day gradually morphed into evening, but the Echoing Enclaves remained abuzz with activity. With each laugh, each shared story, and each virtual journey, NeoVille's residents were not only witnessing the world but becoming an integral part of its ever-evolving narrative. The city was no longer an isolated bubble of progress; it was a vibrant mosaic of global echoes, harmonizing in unity and shared aspirations.

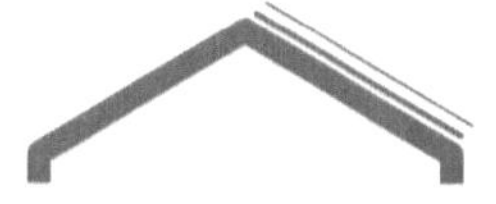

CHAPTER THIRTY-FIVE

Wisdom Weaves

Downtown NeoVille was agog with excitement. "Wisdom Weaves," an initiative aimed at bridging generations through shared knowledge, was launching today. The concept was groundbreaking: a digital realm where the city's seniors would share stories, life lessons, traditions, and skills with younger generations.

Amidst the hustle and bustle, Mrs. Walker, an octogenarian with a twinkle in her eye, sat comfortably in a state-of-the-art digital booth, preparing to share her experience of growing up in a pre-digital era. Curious teens gathered around, eager to dive deep into tales of a world devoid of the technological wonders they took for granted.

"I remember," Mrs. Walker began, her voice strong yet filled with nostalgia, "when letters were our only means of long-distance communication. The joy of receiving handwritten notes, the scent of the paper, the wait—it taught us patience and the art of heartfelt expression."

Across the hall, a holographic representation of an ancient bazaar was set up. Mr. Patel, a retired merchant, held court, recounting tales of age-old trade practices, the art of negotiation, and the importance of human relationships in business. Young entrepreneurs listened raptly, realizing that beneath the digital advancements, the essence of trade remained unchanged.

Aria, watching the interactions, mused aloud, "It's fascinating. While our city leaps into the future, these stories anchor us. They remind us of our roots."

Liam, engrossed in a session about traditional dance forms, responded, "It's a balance, isn't it? As we propel forward, drawing from the past ensures we don't lose our essence. This weaving of wisdom gives us perspective."

Elara, engaging with a group learning ancient meditation techniques, added, "It's more than just stories and skills. It's a way of thinking, a mindset. These sessions teach us resilience, adaptability, and the art of thriving amidst adversities."

The most remarkable aspect of Wisdom Weaves was the Digital Memory Lane—a corridor where seniors could upload memories, experiences, and knowledge into an interactive cloud. This virtual space allowed users to "walk" through varied life experiences, feeling the emotions and learning the lessons firsthand.

By evening, as NeoVille's skyline lit up, Wisdom Weaves had transformed from an event to a movement. The conversations extended beyond the designated zones. Parks, cafes, and even homes resonated with tales of yore and discussions on how they could be integrated into NeoVille's future fabric.

It wasn't just an exchange between generations; it was a harmonious blend of the past and the future. The weaves of wisdom were no longer tales told but lessons lived, ensuring that as NeoVille hurtled towards tomorrow, the echoes of yesterday remained firmly embedded in its soul.

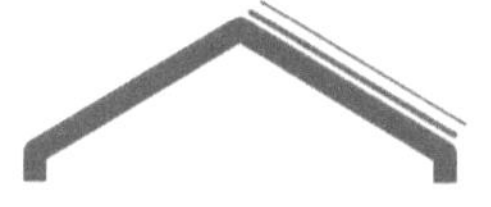

CHAPTER THIRTY-SIX

Fractals of Fusion

The following week introduced an avant-garde concept to NeoVille: The Fractal Fairgrounds. It wasn't a mere amusement park or an exhibition. It was a dynamic zone where art, science, culture, and technology converged, creating ripples of fusion.

At the fair's entrance stood a magnificent installation—a colossal tree made entirely of shimmering holographic lights. Each branch represented a different facet of knowledge, and visitors could interact with its shimmering leaves, absorbing information and sharing their own insights.

Liam was particularly drawn to a booth labeled "Musical Fractals." Here, traditional instruments from around the world were merged with digital soundscapes, creating a symphony that transcended geographical boundaries. He watched as a Japanese Koto harmonized with African Djembes, and a digital backdrop morphed in response to the melodies, weaving patterns that told tales of unity.

Aria, ever the artist, was engrossed in the "Chromatic Cultures" section. It featured palettes inspired by different global regions. Participants could create art using these palettes, and AI would then combine the diverse pieces, producing a masterpiece that encapsulated the essence of global unity.

Elsewhere, Elara found herself amidst "Gastronomic Galaxies", where chefs amalgamated culinary traditions, creating dishes that tasted like home, no matter where one hailed from. A Thai curry infused with Mexican spices or a French patisserie with hints of Indian cardamom showcased the magic of blending boundaries.

One of the most profound zones was the "Digital Diaries". Here, residents could record their daily experiences, struggles, and achievements in NeoVille. These stories were then algorithmically blended to create a digital narrative—a fluid, ever-evolving story representing collective city experiences.

As the sun began its descent, casting the fairgrounds in a golden hue, a grand spectacle began at the center stage. An amalgamation of dance forms, from ballet to bharatanatyam, took center stage. Yet, it wasn't just the movements that captivated; it was the stories they told—stories of shared struggles, jubilations, dreams, and the undeniable human spirit that binds all.

By nightfall, as stars painted the skies and the shimmering tree installation bathed NeoVille in an ethereal glow, a realization dawned upon its residents. They were living amidst a fusion, not just of cultures or technologies, but of aspirations and dreams. The fractals, though varied and distinct, came together to form a coherent picture—a vision of a unified future, intricately interwoven by the threads of the past and the present.

The Fractals of Fusion, it turned out, wasn't just an event. It was a reflection of NeoVille itself—a city where every individual, memory, and dream formed an essential fragment of a mesmerizing mosaic.

CHAPTER THIRTY-SEVEN

The Global Guild

A new sun rose, and with it came an exciting announcement for the residents of NeoVille. The city had been chosen as the inaugural location for "The Global Guild," an international council established to share knowledge, technology, and cultural practices among the future cities of the world.

The Guild's establishment was a recognition that while each city was unique, the challenges they faced were often similar. By fostering collaboration and understanding, they aimed to make every city better prepared for the future.

NeoVille's Confluence Hall, an architectural marvel combining elements from various world cultures, was selected as the meeting ground. Delegates from different future cities arrived, bringing with them the vibrancy, experiences, and wisdom of their metropolises.

Elara, being at the forefront of technology, was invited to present NeoVille's accomplishments in merging traditional and digital art forms. She was also curious about innovations from other cities. A delegate from AquaUtopia demonstrated their breakthroughs in underwater living and sustainable seafood farming. Meanwhile, a representative from SkyLands discussed their cloud-based transport systems and aerial agricultural practices.

Liam and Aria were volunteers, assisting in organizing cultural showcases each evening. From dance performances that defied gravity to music that resonated with the universe's frequencies, these evenings became a celebration of human ingenuity and shared cultural richness.

However, the Guild's highlight was the creation of a Digital Collaboration Network or DCN. This platform allowed cities to upload challenges they were facing, and others could propose solutions, share resources, or provide expertise. For instance, when TerraVille uploaded about their soil degradation issue, NeoVille's agricultural tech team offered an AI solution they had been working on.

Each city had its digital corner in the DCN, acting as a virtual embassy. Residents of NeoVille could stroll through these virtual spaces, absorbing information, attending workshops, or simply interacting with global counterparts.

The week culminated in the signing of the Neo Pact – a commitment from all cities to share knowledge, support in crises, and, most importantly, to uphold the principles of unity, sustainability, and cultural respect.

As the delegates departed, they left behind more than just technological innovations and solutions. They imprinted NeoVille with stories, memories, and a renewed sense of global camaraderie.

The Global Guild wasn't just a meeting; it was a movement. A movement that signaled the start of a harmonious global society, a world where cities stood not in competition but in collaboration, crafting a brighter, shared future.

CHAPTER THIRTY-EIGHT

Cultural Codex

Amidst the myriad developments in NeoVille, a subtle yet significant initiative took root: The Cultural Codex. A massive digital archive, it was more than just a database—it was an ever-evolving tapestry of human cultures, traditions, and stories from around the world. Its inception was sparked by the collaborations and exchanges from The Global Guild.

The heart of the Codex was its immersive experience. Donning specialized visors, visitors could walk through historical periods, witness significant events, or even partake in traditional ceremonies. The memories of elders from around the globe were digitized, ensuring that stories passed down through generations found a permanent place in this digital haven.

Liam was instrumental in creating interactive sections for younger visitors. Children could virtually travel to different countries, learn native dances, or cook traditional dishes right beside virtual grandmas and grandpas, experiencing the warmth of familial teachings.

Aria, meanwhile, led an initiative titled "Colors of Culture." This visual journey showcased global art forms, from the intricacies of Aboriginal dot paintings to the swirling patterns of Alpona from

India. Viewers could create collaborative art, merging two or more cultural styles, symbolizing the unity in diversity.

Elara's tech team built the "Tales in Tones" segment. Here, languages from the world played like music. Visitors could hear poetry, lullabies, or proverbs in hundreds of languages, understanding not just the words, but the emotions they conveyed. There was also an AI tutor, which could teach basic phrases or greetings from any chosen language.

But what truly set the Cultural Codex apart was its "Living Legacy" section. Here, individuals could record and share their own stories, personal traditions, or family customs. These individual threads would then be woven into the larger tapestry, ensuring that every voice, no matter how seemingly small, found its place in the grand narrative.

Word of the Codex spread globally. Schools started virtual field trips, families shared their ancestries, and researchers found a treasure trove of data. The Codex became a bridge connecting the past and the future, ensuring that while society embraced technological advances, it remained firmly rooted in its diverse and rich heritage.

By the end of the month, NeoVille had another landmark, not of towering steel or shimmering holographs, but of stories, emotions, and the shared journey of humanity. The Cultural Codex stood as a testament to the belief that while technology could build cities, it was culture and shared stories that truly built civilizations.

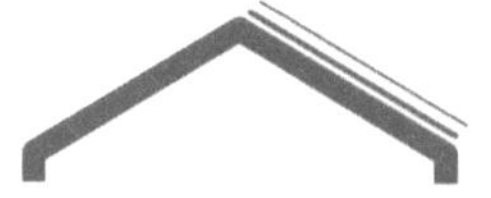

CHAPTER THIRTY-NINE

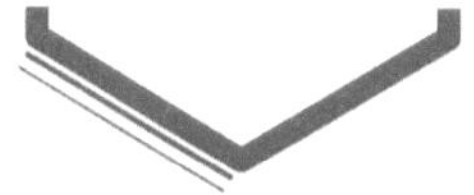

Holistic Hues

NeoVille's creative energy pulsed through every corner, but at the heart of its artistic revolution lay a unique project called "Holistic Hues." The brainchild of Maya, an artist who had risen to prominence within the city, it was an attempt to unite various art forms into a single, cohesive masterpiece.

Maya believed that art had the power to transcend mediums, evoking emotions that transcended words. She envisioned a living gallery, a place where visitors would physically experience the essence of NeoVille's spirit.

Aria and Liam had been invited to contribute, each drawn to the project's ambition. Aria saw it as a canvas of human emotions, while Liam, as a tech genius, saw it as an opportunity to blend art and innovation in ways never before seen.

The exhibition was set in an expansive gallery within NeoVille's Cultural Quarter. The walls were adorned with paintings, sculptures, and digital installations. The air was rich with the scent of fresh flowers, their presence integral to the sensory experience.

As visitors entered, they were handed small, high-tech devices that resembled paintbrushes. These devices were programmed to interact with the artworks, responding to colors, textures, and emotions.

Aria's section featured intricate paintings, each resonating with a unique emotion. Visitors could "paint" with their devices, mixing hues to create their own emotional masterpieces. They could step into her art, experiencing empathy, joy, or nostalgia as if it were their own.

Liam's section delved into the fusion of art and technology. His holographic installations created illusions that pushed the boundaries of reality. Visitors could interact with the digital art, turning colors into music, textures into stories. The gallery itself became a living, breathing entity, adapting to the participants' thoughts and emotions.

In the heart of the gallery, Maya's centerpiece was a colossal sculpture. It was a unity of all the art forms, an embodiment of NeoVille's harmonious spirit. Visitors could touch it, and their emotions were translated into a symphony of light, sound, and fragrance. It was a testament to Maya's vision and the collaboration of countless artists.

As the exhibition reached its zenith, Aria and Liam stood together, watching people move through the gallery. Their individual contributions had become threads woven into the vibrant tapestry of Holistic Hues.

"Aria, Liam, you've truly brought life to this place," Maya whispered, her eyes shining with gratitude.

Liam smiled, looking at Aria. "It's amazing how art can transcend boundaries, isn't it?"

Aria nodded, her gaze on the interactive artwork. "And technology can amplify its impact."

As the last visitor left the gallery, the trio remained, basking in the echoes of an experience that was more than art—it was a testament to NeoVille's evolving spirit, where innovation, art, and emotion danced in perfect synergy.

CHAPTER FORTY

Celestial Celebrations

The grand culmination of NeoVille's artistic renaissance was fast approaching. The city was buzzing with excitement as the final event, "Celestial Celebrations," was about to unfold. This event was more than just a closing ceremony; it was a spectacular showcase of NeoVille's transformation into a hub of innovation, art, and unity.

The venue was the sprawling Central Square, transformed into a dreamlike space with floating installations, holographic projections, and cascading fountains of light. Guests from all walks of life, including artists, technologists, and citizens, gathered to witness NeoVille's shining moment.

The night sky was clear, and stars twinkled like diamonds above, reflecting the city's spirit. The event commenced with an ethereal musical performance. The sound of traditional instruments merged seamlessly with digital symphonies, creating an otherworldly ambiance.

Liam and Aria, having played integral roles in NeoVille's transformation, were honored guests. They stood together at the heart of the celebrations, representing the seamless synergy between art and technology.

Solara took the stage, her voice resonating through the square. "Welcome, everyone, to Celestial Celebrations—a night of magic, creativity, and unity. NeoVille's journey has been one of innovation and collaboration, where dreams have woven themselves into our very fabric."

As Solara spoke, holographic displays illuminated the square, projecting images of NeoVille's milestones. The audience was transported through time, reliving the city's evolution from its inception to this moment.

Aria stepped forward, her eyes sparkling with emotion. "In this city, art has become a canvas of emotions, a thread connecting hearts. Our stories, dreams, and colors have converged to create a symphony that resonates with every individual."

Liam followed, his voice steady yet passionate. "And technology has been our tool to bridge gaps, break barriers, and amplify our creations. It's a testament to the fact that when art and technology unite, incredible things happen."

As they finished speaking, a breathtaking holographic display enveloped the square. It was a living representation of NeoVille's essence—a fusion of colors, light, and sound that danced in harmony. The crowd was awestruck, their applause echoing like thunder.

The night continued with performances that blended physical and digital art, music that resonated with the heartbeat of the city, and interactive installations that allowed the audience to become part of the art itself.

As the event reached its crescendo, a shower of holographic fireworks burst across the sky. It was as if the stars themselves were celebrating NeoVille's triumph.

Aria and Liam stood side by side, gazing up at the spectacle. "We did it," Aria whispered, her voice a mix of awe and contentment.

Liam nodded, his heart full. "Together, we truly did."

And as the last notes of music faded into the night, NeoVille's spirit soared higher than ever before. The city that had once faced uncertainty had emerged as a beacon of unity, artistry, and innovation—a testament to the potential of human collaboration and the boundless power of dreams.

Part Five

Horizons of Hope

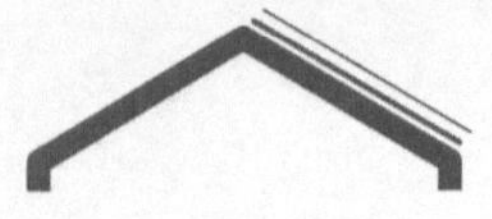

CHAPTER FORTY-ONE

Aria's Ascent

The city of NeoVille was abuzz with excitement. Today marked the inauguration of the "NeoVille Visionary Summit", a global conference aiming to showcase and share the innovations and progress made by the city with the world. Leaders, thinkers, and pioneers from all spheres of life were flocking in, their ships dotting the NeoVille sky.

But the highlight was yet to come. Aria, the once reticent artist who found her voice amidst the canvas of unity, was chosen to deliver the keynote address. Her journey, mirroring NeoVille's transformative tale, had made her a beacon of hope and inspiration for many.

Stepping onto the dais set against the backdrop of the sprawling city skyline, Aria took a deep breath. The multitude of faces, some familiar, others new, all turned to her in anticipation.

"Once, NeoVille was just a canvas – empty, yet brimming with potential. Just like every blank page or every silent studio waiting for the first stroke of a brush, the first note of a song. And just like every artist, we had our doubts, our fears," she began, her voice resonating with emotion.

She narrated her personal journey, from the uncertain artist seeking validation in a virtual world to becoming an emblem of

NeoVille's transformative spirit. She spoke of Liam, her anchor, and of the countless souls who had rallied behind the dream of a harmonious future.

"With every brushstroke, with every pixel, we created not just art, but a movement. A movement that went beyond borders, transcending digital realms and physical terrains."

But Aria's message went deeper than just the success tale of NeoVille. She delved into the challenges the world was grappling with - rising inequalities, the blurring lines between the real and virtual, and the ethical quandaries of rapid technological advancements.

As her address drew to a close, Aria unveiled her latest masterpiece. A holographic projection sprang to life above her, showcasing a planet where cities reminiscent of NeoVille dotted the landscapes. "This," she declared, "is a vision of a world united. Not just by technology, but by dreams, by hope."

The applause was deafening. The image of that hopeful world, coupled with Aria's words, ignited a flame in every heart. It was evident - NeoVille was no longer just a city. It had become a symbol, a beacon guiding the world towards newer horizons of hope.

CHAPTER FORTY-TWO

Liam's Luminance

The days following Aria's address were a whirlwind. The NeoVille Visionary Summit was in full swing, with delegations from around the world pouring into the city to experience its marvels firsthand. Among the many discussions, forums, and workshops, there was one event in particular that had garnered unparalleled anticipation: Liam's showcase.

Liam had always been the silent strength behind the scenes, orchestrating the harmony between digital and real. But in this summit, he was to step into the limelight with his creation, a groundbreaking platform that was rumored to revolutionize the way the world connected.

In the heart of NeoVille's grand convention center, a stage bathed in gentle, pulsating lights awaited Liam. As he emerged, the room's energy shifted palpably. The unassuming, ever-supportive best friend of Aria had his moment, and the audience knew they were about to witness something extraordinary.

With a humble nod, Liam began, "Every generation has its language. Ours is binary and brushstrokes, pixels and palettes. Today, I present to you the culmination of years of endeavor—a platform that understands this language and uses it to bridge minds and souls."

With a dramatic flourish, screens around the hall came to life, displaying an interface that seemed to blend digital aesthetics with organic fluidity. "Luminance," Liam announced, "is our beacon into the future."

Luminance was no ordinary platform. It was an ecosystem, an expansive digital realm where art, technology, and human experiences converged. It allowed artists to collaborate in real-time, creating masterpieces that resonated with shared human experiences, irrespective of geographic or cultural divides.

More than that, Luminance had inbuilt AI systems that studied global artistic trends and provided insights, ensuring that art was not just an expression but also a dialogue—a dialogue that transcended languages and borders.

As Liam showcased the features, the audience was in awe. Artists could share their emotions, and the platform would find the perfect collaborator from any corner of the globe, someone who resonated with those emotions, creating unity in creation like never before.

But Liam's brilliance wasn't just in creating Luminance; it was in ensuring that it was accessible to all. "Art," he proclaimed, "is the birthright of every soul. Luminance is free, open to every individual who seeks to share, collaborate, or simply experience."

The standing ovation that followed was testament to NeoVille's spirit. It celebrated innovators, dreamers, and believers. And that day, it celebrated Liam, whose luminance promised a world where dreams could be woven together, creating a tapestry of hope for tomorrow.

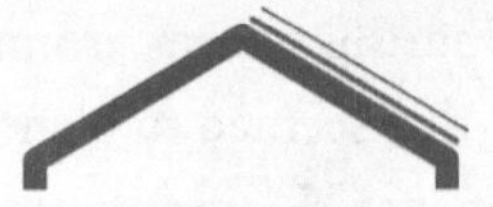

CHAPTER FORTY-THREE

NeoVille Nurtures

NeoVille had always been a city that valued both its past and its future. Every brick and byte of the city pulsed with stories of visionaries who had dared to dream. But beyond the technology and the innovation, what truly made NeoVille stand apart was its commitment to nurturing the soul. And that ethos came to the forefront as the city embarked on its most ambitious project yet.

The NeoVille Nurtures initiative was announced on a bright, sunny morning. Aria and Liam, standing side by side on the main stage, presented their vision of a city that went beyond its digital marvels. Their vision was to create spaces and platforms where individuals could grow, not just technologically, but emotionally and spiritually.

"We've integrated our lives with technology," Aria began, her voice filled with warmth. "But what's more important is how we integrate our hearts with each other. NeoVille Nurtures is our commitment to that integration."

Liam continued, "We're creating spaces throughout the city where individuals can come to learn, to share, and most importantly, to grow. These spaces are open to everyone, irrespective of their background, age, or skills. Here, an artist can learn coding, a technologist can pick up a paintbrush, and a child can dream uninhibited."

As part of the initiative, 'Nurture Hubs' were launched across NeoVille. These were centers equipped with the latest technology, but they also housed libraries, art studios, music rooms, and meditation zones. They were places where technology met tranquility, and creativity met code.

Each hub was manned by mentors, individuals who had excelled in their respective fields. They were there not to instruct but to guide, to provide a helping hand to those who sought knowledge.

But what truly set NeoVille Nurtures apart was its emphasis on mental health. Each hub housed counselors and therapists, ensuring that as the city soared to new digital heights, its residents remained grounded, their mental well-being always prioritized.

The response was overwhelming. NeoVille's residents flocked to these hubs. Stories emerged of friendships forged, of passions discovered, and of dreams realized. A retired teacher picked up virtual reality design, a teenager found solace in classical music, and a businessman rediscovered his love for poetry.

As days turned into weeks, NeoVille Nurtures became more than just an initiative; it became a movement. It epitomized the essence of NeoVille—a city that wasn't just smart but also soulful, always striving to create a tomorrow where every individual could find their true calling.

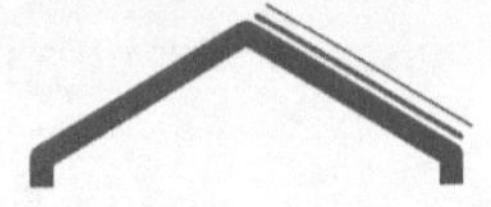

CHAPTER FORTY-FOUR

Visions and Ventures

NeoVille's central plaza was abuzz with activity, hosting the city's first-ever "Visionary Venture Fair." This event, conceptualized as a part of NeoVille Nurtures, was an attempt to bring together the city's brightest minds with young dreamers. The plaza was adorned with holographic banners and vibrant lights, giving a luminescent glow to the evening sky.

Various booths and stalls lined the plaza, each representing a unique venture rooted in the balance of technology and humanity. There was a booth that showcased an app to help the visually impaired experience art, another demonstrating a new communication tool for the differently-abled, and a group that brought together elderly storytellers with young tech enthusiasts to digitize and immortalize their tales.

Aria, dressed in a smart jumpsuit with futuristic patterns, stood watching as people interacted with the booths. She observed a group of school children getting animated explanations from an elder, both sides equally excited. It was visions like these that she had dreamt of—generations merging, technology bridging gaps, and pure human connection.

Liam, with a holographic badge that read 'Guest Speaker', approached her. "You know," he began, taking a deep breath, "I've been part of numerous tech conferences and innovation summits. But this... this is something else."

Aria smiled, "It's the heart, Liam. Every venture here isn't just a business model; it's a dream, a passion, a vision for a better world."

Their attention was diverted by a sudden applause. At the center of the plaza, a stage had been set up for pitches. A young girl, no older than fifteen, stood confidently as she presented her vision: a platform where youngsters could be paired with senior citizens to learn skills and crafts that were slowly fading away. It wasn't just about preserving traditions but also about fostering friendships across generations.

As the day transitioned into evening, more visionaries took the stage, their ventures echoing the core principle of NeoVille Nurtures: progress with heart. There were innovations in clean energy, art-tech integrations, and platforms that promoted mental wellness. Every pitch resonated with hope, determination, and the desire to make a meaningful impact.

When the fair concluded, the plaza was illuminated with drones forming patterns in the sky, symbolizing unity, progress, and hope. Aria and Liam, standing side by side, looked up, their hearts full. NeoVille was more than just a city; it was an ever-evolving testament to humanity's best aspirations.

Liam whispered, "This is the future, Aria. Not just technology for the sake of it, but technology that uplifts, nurtures, and brings us closer."

Aria nodded, "It's not just visions; it's ventures that change the world."

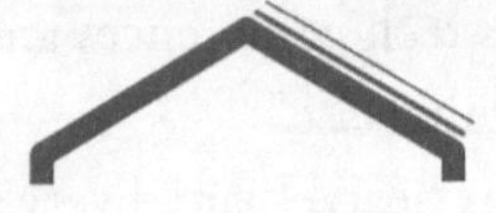

CHAPTER FORTY-FIVE

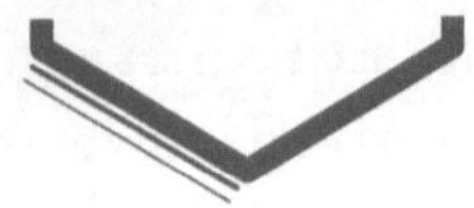

Ethereal Embrace

The streets of NeoVille were silent, punctuated only by the gentle hum of passing autonomous vehicles and the soft, lilting sounds of ethereal music that emanated from various corners. Tonight was the "Ethereal Embrace" night, an annual event where the city's inhabitants were encouraged to disconnect from the digital and reconnect with their emotions, the environment, and each other.

Aria stood on her apartment balcony, which overlooked the serene NeoVille lake. The waters reflected the city's muted lights and above, drones released luminescent particles that danced in the night sky, mimicking a cascade of stars. Each particle, when inhaled, induced a state of mild euphoria, enabling people to truly feel their surroundings and emotions.

The idea behind the "Ethereal Embrace" was to immerse oneself in natural sensations and remember the beauty of unfiltered, raw human connection. While NeoVille was at the pinnacle of technological advancements, its founders recognized the importance of balance.

Liam, having been invited by Aria to share this experience, joined her on the balcony. They inhaled the luminescent particles, feeling a warmth spread through them, bringing clarity and amplifying their senses. The city noises faded, replaced by the soft sound of their own breathing and the distant, comforting lullaby of nature.

Holding hands, they ventured into the streets where people were engrossed in various activities—couples danced to the city's soft music, families picnicked under holographic trees, and others simply lay on the grass, stargazing.

They reached a park where a circle had been formed. In its center, a woman played a traditional harp, its music seeming to speak directly to the soul. Around her, people sat with closed eyes, meditating or simply losing themselves in the melody. Aria and Liam joined them, sitting close, their fingers intertwined.

As the harpist played, her music took them on a journey, evoking memories of their past, dreams of their future, and the profound beauty of the present. It was a reminder of the delicate tapestry of human experience, where moments of pain and joy, loss and discovery, were interwoven.

When the music ceased, a palpable silence lingered. People slowly opened their eyes, their faces reflecting deep introspection. Some had tears, some smiles, and others a serene expression of contentment.

The duo walked back, hand in hand, through the now awakening city. As dawn approached, the ethereal particles faded, and the digital realm began to regain its prominence. But the essence of the night remained, a gentle reminder of the balance between progress and preserving the core of what makes us human.

"That was... transcendent," Liam whispered.

Aria nodded, squeezing his hand, "A night to remember that amidst all our advances, it's these moments of pure, unadulterated connection that truly matter."

In a city where tomorrow was constantly being crafted, tonight had been a tribute to timeless emotions, an ethereal embrace of humanity's core.

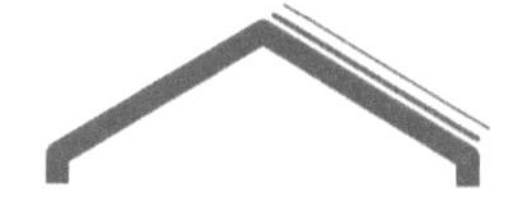

CHAPTER FORTY-SIX

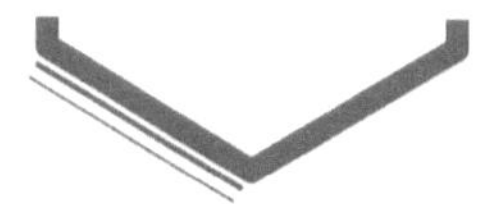

The Crucible of Creation

NeoVille's grand auditorium was filled to the brim. The Crucible of Creation was an event that the inhabitants of the city waited for all year. It was not just an event; it was a movement. It was a day where people from all walks of life came together to present their most groundbreaking innovations, artistic expressions, and philosophical insights. It was where dreams transformed into tangible realities.

Aria and Liam were among the presenters, having worked on an idea that fused their unique skills and visions. Their project aimed at harnessing the power of collective memories, stories, and emotions to shape the virtual landscapes of NeoVille, making the digital realm more human-centric.

The stage was awash with lights of varying hues, creating an aura of anticipation. Holographic displays showcased intricate details of the presentations. It was a confluence of the traditional and the avant-garde.

An AI emcee, designed to radiate warmth and charisma, began the proceedings. "Ladies, gentlemen, and esteemed guests, welcome to the Crucible of Creation. Today, you'll witness the birth of ideas that could shape our tomorrows."

The presentations were diverse. There was an invention that could transform water from the atmosphere into potable drinking water using minimal energy. Another group showcased a digital art installation where viewers could step into historic moments, experiencing them first-hand.

Finally, it was Aria and Liam's turn. The stage transformed into a living mural of memories and dreams, echoing the themes of their earlier adventures. Images of their journey through NeoVille, their challenges, and their triumphs filled the space.

Aria began, "In a world where our reality is increasingly shaped by bytes and pixels, we wanted to introduce something deeply human into the mix: our collective memories."

Liam continued, "Imagine a cityscape that evolves with our stories, our hopes, our fears. A building might wear the colors of a sunset remembered from childhood. A park could echo with the laughter of a first date."

As they spoke, the audience could see and feel those memories. The atmosphere was thick with emotion — nostalgia, joy, sorrow, hope. It was as if the entire city was breathing, alive with the heartbeat of its inhabitants.

Their presentation concluded with a live demo. Volunteers from the audience came up, shared a memory, and watched as a section of NeoVille's virtual representation transformed in real-time, reflecting that memory.

The applause was thunderous. But more than the applause, it was the tears, the smiles, the hugs, and the conversations that followed which spoke volumes. NeoVille wasn't just a city of the future; it was a crucible where the human spirit was constantly being redefined and reborn.

As the event wrapped up, Aria and Liam stepped out into the night, their hearts full. They had not only showcased an idea but had also sparked a movement, one that recognized the importance of preserving and celebrating human essence in a rapidly digitizing world. The Crucible of Creation wasn't just an event; it was the soul of NeoVille, reminding everyone of the power of collective creation.

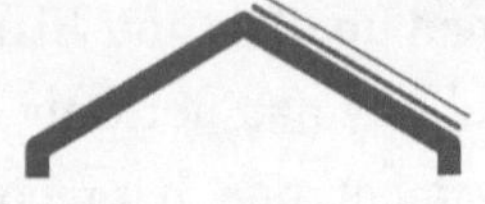

CHAPTER FORTY-SEVEN

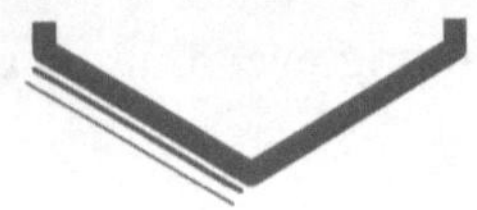

Unified Universe

In the wake of the Crucible of Creation, NeoVille was abuzz with conversations about Aria and Liam's groundbreaking initiative. Their project had become more than just a presentation—it was a symbol of unity, bridging the gaps between the digital and the real, between the past and the future.

The Mayor of NeoVille, a forward-thinking leader named Solara, decided to host a grand symposium in the heart of the city. She envisioned it as a platform to discuss and actualize the integration of these "living memories" into the very fabric of NeoVille. The event would be called "Unified Universe."

Aria, Liam, and other key innovators were invited as guest speakers. The symposium would be open to all citizens, allowing everyone to be part of this groundbreaking moment in NeoVille's history.

Under the gleaming neo-lights, the city center was transformed into a spectacular arena. Holographic screens floated in the air, and AI-driven drones captured every moment, broadcasting it across NeoVille and beyond.

Solara took the stage, her voice echoing with excitement. "Welcome to the dawn of a new era! Today, we discuss not just the future of our city but of humanity. The 'Unified Universe' project is our answer to a world fragmented by technology. We're building bridges, not barriers."

Aria and Liam followed with a demonstration. They showcased how every person could contribute to this digital tapestry. From an elderly man's tales of the old world to a child's dreams of future galaxies, the virtual landscape of NeoVille transformed with every story.

As the day progressed, workshops were held on the potential applications of this technology. Educators spoke about interactive classrooms where history came alive. Urban planners discussed creating flexible city zones that evolved with citizens' needs and memories. Artists envisioned collaborative masterpieces, bringing together the aspirations of thousands.

However, it wasn't just about the grand ideas. Intimate corners of the venue were dedicated to personal stories. People sat together, some strangers, some friends, and shared anecdotes, dreams, and hopes. The air was thick with laughter, tears, and the palpable excitement of a shared future.

The culmination of the event was a spectacular light show. The skies of NeoVille shimmered as memories, both old and new, played out above, turning the city into a mesmerizing canvas of collective human experience.

As the lights dimmed, Solara's voice resonated once more. "Today, we've taken a step closer to unity, reminding ourselves that while technology can shape our future, it's our shared stories and memories that truly define us."

And as NeoVille slept that night, it wasn't just a city of lights and technology; it was a living, breathing testament to humanity's enduring spirit and the hope of a truly unified universe.

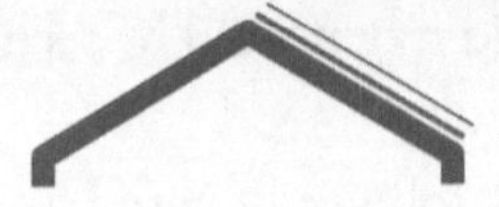

CHAPTER FORTY-EIGHT

Mystic Mosaics

A week after the "Unified Universe" symposium, NeoVille was still thrumming with the energy of possibility. While the cityscape had always been vibrant, it was now threaded with a more profound sense of connection. The grand tapestry of shared memories and aspirations was slowly, but surely, becoming interwoven into every digital street, corner, and structure.

Aria and Liam, having garnered immense attention, decided to channel this energy into a tangible symbol of unity. They proposed an art project, one that combined traditional artistry with the digital memories they'd been gathering. They called it "Mystic Mosaics."

Mystic Mosaics would be both an event and a living memorial. Artists and citizens alike were invited to co-create a sprawling mosaic installation at NeoVille's Central Park. This wouldn't be just any artwork; it would integrate real-world, tactile materials with holographic representations of NeoVille's shared memories.

The city administration, seeing the potential of such an endeavor, immediately sanctioned the project. And in no time, Central Park was alive with excitement. Booths were set up with both physical and digital palettes. Artists could pick and choose from both realms, seamlessly merging them into intricate designs.

Aria, a beacon of enthusiasm, hovered around a particular section which celebrated the city's youth. Here, holographic butterflies, born from childhood dreams, flitted around hand-painted flowers. In another corner, Liam worked on representing the elderly of NeoVille, integrating 3D recordings of their laughter and stories with painted silhouettes that shimmered and moved.

As days morphed into nights and back into days, the Mystic Mosaics grew. The once-empty grounds of Central Park were now a dizzying display of stories, art, and innovation. From a distance, it looked like a gigantic quilt, each patch a unique blend of history and future.

The day the project was completed, NeoVille gathered en masse at Central Park. Solara, ever the visionary, initiated the unveiling. As she pulled away the massive digital drapes, gasps filled the air. Before them lay the heart and soul of NeoVille, laid out in vibrant patterns and colors, illuminated by the memories and dreams of its citizens.

Children rushed forward, pointing at butterflies they'd dreamt up. Elders shed tears, recognizing younger versions of themselves woven next to their current visages. Every inch of the Mystic Mosaics told a tale, every corner echoed with emotion.

As the sun set, Aria and Liam stood hand in hand, gazing at their creation. It wasn't just art; it was a testament to the power of collective spirit, a bridge between eras, a tangible reminder that when humanity came together, they could create magic.

And as NeoVille slept under the starlit sky, the Mystic Mosaics pulsed with its own light, a beacon of hope and unity in an ever-evolving world.

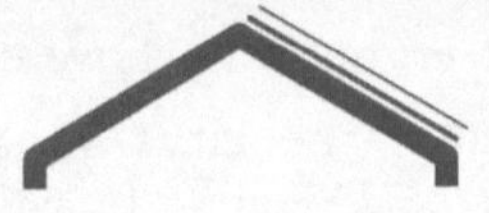

CHAPTER FORTY-NINE

Genesis of Tomorrow

With the Mystic Mosaics as a testament to NeoVille's shared journey, a spark ignited in the hearts of its residents. Aria and Liam, once struggling to find their place, had now become central figures in the city's renaissance. Their narratives of unity and shared experiences were becoming emblematic of the city's direction.

NeoVille began to evolve further, not just technologically but ideologically. It became a city where barriers were actively dismantled. Districts that once only housed artists or technologists now intermingled. There was a surge in collaborative projects, with individuals reaching across their domains of expertise to co-create.

In this environment of burgeoning collaborations, a new venture was born, one that would potentially shape the future: The Genesis Institute.

The Genesis Institute was an ambitious educational institution, an idea conceptualized by Solara with Aria and Liam as its pioneering ambassadors. Its goal was to nurture the next generation, ensuring they grew up in a world where the boundaries between the physical and digital, between various disciplines, were fluid. It aimed to integrate lessons from NeoVille's past with the innovations of its present.

The Institute wasn't just another school. It was an immersive experience. Using advanced AI-driven holographic systems, students could dive deep into historical events, learning from the past. Similarly, they could project potential futures, allowing them to understand the implications of their choices.

Aria took charge of the artistic endeavors at the Institute. Students under her wing painted galaxies, composed music that resonated with one's heartbeat, and created art that told stories, just like the Mystic Mosaics.

Liam, on the other hand, headed the technological wing. But his teachings were unconventional. Instead of just coding and digital designs, Liam emphasized the ethics of creation, the responsibility that came with innovation, and the importance of ensuring technology served humanity and not the other way around.

As months went by, the Genesis Institute became the heart of NeoVille, a place where young minds were shaped to be critical thinkers, innovators, and above all, compassionate individuals.

One evening, as the city lights shimmered, Liam and Aria stood atop the Institute, gazing at the sprawling city. The weight of their journey was evident in their eyes. From feeling lost in a vast digital ocean to shaping the very currents of that ocean, they had come a long way.

"I never imagined we'd be here," Aria whispered, her fingers tracing patterns in the holographic mist surrounding them.

Liam smiled, pulling her close. "This is just the beginning, Aria. We've sown the seeds for the Genesis of Tomorrow."

And as dawn broke, the city that never truly slept continued its dance of evolution, each resident contributing a step, each innovation a beat, all leading towards a harmonious future.

CHAPTER FIFTY

Resonance and Rebirth

A year had passed since the establishment of the Genesis Institute. The echoing resonance of NeoVille's unity and the rebirth of its spirit reverberated far beyond its borders. Cities across the world began looking towards NeoVille as the prototype of harmony between humanity, art, and technology.

Solara's ambitious project, once viewed with skepticism, had transformed into a beacon of inspiration. But the true highlight wasn't the advanced tech or the impressive architecture – it was the people. They had become the living embodiment of NeoVille's spirit.

As the anniversary of the Institute approached, a grand gala was planned. The entire city was abuzz with excitement, and guests from far and wide were set to attend. Central to the event was an unveiling - a collaborative artwork that Aria, Liam, and many others had been working on in secret for months.

The night of the gala arrived, illuminated by NeoVille's spectacular luminescent skyline. Dignitaries, artists, tech wizards, and residents gathered, their collective anticipation palpable.

Liam and Aria took the stage, hand in hand. Behind them stood a massive canvas covered in a shimmering drape.

"As NeoVille's journey continues," began Aria, "we've learned that our strength doesn't lie in just our individual abilities, but in our collective spirit."

Liam continued, "Tonight, we unveil not just an artwork, but a symbol. A testament to our unity, our growth, and our shared vision."

With a dramatic flourish, they pulled away the drape. The audience gasped in awe.

It wasn't a static painting or a digital display. It was a living tapestry, a seamless fusion of art and technology. Scenes from NeoVille's past, its challenges, its victories, its dreams, and its aspirations flowed across the canvas. Every individual in the city could find a piece of their story woven into the vast narrative. It pulsed, resonated, and breathed with life.

Tears streamed down Solara's face as she realized her dream was no longer just a dream. NeoVille was alive, its heartbeat strong and steady.

The gala went on, but the tapestry became its focal point. People from diverse backgrounds and professions discussed, debated, and dreamt together in its presence, inspired by its message.

As the first rays of dawn began to break, the party showed no signs of slowing down. Liam, Aria, and Solara stood together, watching their city celebrate.

"We did it," whispered Solara, her voice choked with emotion.

Aria smiled, her eyes sparkling with tears. "No, *we* did it. All of us. Together."

Liam nodded, wrapping his arms around them both. "To resonance and rebirth."

The trio looked out over NeoVille, the city of dreams reborn, its future brighter than ever.

To Aria,

Hey Aria,

Do you remember painting under the oak tree? I still laugh thinking about my lopsided mountains. You taught me to find beauty in imperfections. I often sketch you lost in your art, your laughter, your dreams. You inspire me, more than words can tell.

Thank you for the dragon painting. It's by my bedside, reminding me of our shared adventures. Please never stop painting and dreaming, Aria. The world needs your vision.

Grateful for our friendship,

Liam

Beyond the Horizon

The tales of NeoVille traveled like ripples across a pond, touching shores both near and far. Its legend was not just of advanced technology or artistic marvels, but of unity, hope, and the testament of human spirit to overcome adversity. Communities worldwide adopted the spirit of collaboration that NeoVille exemplified.

Liam's workshops expanded globally. A new generation grew up understanding the delicate balance between the real and the virtual, ensuring that technology augmented human experiences, rather than replacing them.

Aria's art installations became sites of pilgrimage, with art enthusiasts, tech moguls, and common citizens all finding solace and inspiration in her work. The intertwined stories of Aria and Liam became almost legendary, representing the harmonious dance between the arts and sciences.

Solara's Genesis Institute emerged as a global powerhouse in education and innovation, a beacon for those looking to meld creativity with technology. It became a hub for visionary thinkers from all domains to come together, craft solutions, and shape the future.

But NeoVille's legacy was even broader. It became synonymous with hope, demonstrating that when faced with challenges, humanity could unite, adapt, and rise.

Years later, at the heart of NeoVille, children would stand before the living tapestry unveiled that gala night, their faces reflecting its luminous glow. They listened, wide-eyed, to tales of the city's transformation - stories of adversity, unity, innovation, and rebirth.

And as the sun set, casting long shadows across NeoVille's gleaming towers and bustling streets, a new generation dreamed of their own mark on the horizon. The spirit of NeoVille - resilience, collaboration, and hope - was eternal.

Don't miss out!

Visit the website below and you can sign up to receive emails whenever Michael A. Garcia publishes a new book. There's no charge and no obligation.

https://books2read.com/r/B-A-CXMAB-CYDOC

Connecting independent readers to independent writers.

About the Author

Michael A. Garcia is a standout figure in the vast world of science fiction. His unique ability to craft stories that teeter between reality and fantasy has cemented his place within the Nexa Novels community. His journey into writing was sparked by the myriad of stories and books his mother shared with him, fanning the flames of his imagination. The cherished family tales, shared across generations, have deeply instilled in him a passion for storytelling. His works delve into the profound intersections of technology's impact on our future while celebrating the enduring spirit of humanity. Every piece from Garcia is both a nod to his roots and a vision of what's on the horizon.

Read more at https://nexanovels.com/.